The Italian Connection

John Keeman

Ringwood Publishing

Glasgow

First published in Scotland in 2015
by
Ringwood Publishing
7 Kirklee Quadrant, Glasgow G12 0TS
www.ringwoodpublishing.com
e-mail mail@ringwoodpublishing.com

ISBN 978-1-901514-20-9
British Library Cataloguing-in Publication Data
A catalogue record for this book is available from the
British Library

Typeset in Times New Roman 11
Printed and bound in the UK
by Lonsdale Direct Solutions

Acknowledgements

My sincere thanks to the Giles family; Ann, Vivien and George, whose late father's writings inspired this book. Thanks also to my friends Ray Urie and Janice Burrows who agreed to read the original manuscript, for a small fee. Appreciation also goes to my publisher for taking a chance on an aged author's debut novel and my editor Keara Donnachie for her patience and helpful contributions.

About the author

John Keeman was born on Finnieston Street, Glasgow on the 28th April, 1944. His father, also John, was a shipyard worker and his mother Jeannie was a one-eyed tearoom waitress. He attended Finnieston Street Primary and Woodside Secondary, where he was a below average pupil with high absence rate. Despite this, John graduated with 2.1 Honours degree in Law and Public Administration at the age of fifty from Glasgow Caledonian University. He has worked various jobs, from coalman to Research Manager for BBC Information. The Italian Connection is John's first novel and he has also written many radio dramas.

Dedication

This book is dedicated to the real George Giles
(1918–2000)

CHAPTER ONE

I woke alone, in what appeared to be a ward in a hospital – but it was unlike any hospital room I'd been in before. The other bed on my right (which I supposed was the same as the one I was lying upon) was a strange-looking contraption. From where I lay, it looked like a cantilever bridge. It had a series of criss-cross tubular bars, small wheels, levers and knobs, all of which allowed for the height to be adjusted and the occupant to be tilted back and forward. Strange-looking it may have been, but it was very comfortable and far removed from the horsehair-stuffed mattresses I was used to sleeping on in my army billet.

Most other things in the room were equally unfamiliar, including a bank of what I took to be television screens: lined up like the eyes of a giant spider, staring down at me from the shelving high on the walls. Television was a new innovation, I remembered. It was being developed just before the war started, but the BBC suspended the service in 1939. I'd only read about this new phenomenon and had never actually seen one, apart from a picture in a newspaper article that accompanied the story about this 'new radio with pictures', as the writer had described it. I knew that a television could show moving pictures like the cinema, but that was the extent of my knowledge.

I didn't see any pictures on the screens, but I appeared to be connected to some of them by a series of fine wires attached to my chest and held in place by a substance like a yellow jelly. I traced the path of the wires with my eyes as far as I could, until they vanished into the back of one of the boxes and I watched, quite fascinated, as a small blip bounced along a line on the screen until I realised it was replicating my heartbeat.

None of what I was witnessing made any sense; neither did the thin, clear tubing that was attached to my arm by a needle and extended above my head into a bag of yellow fluid suspended from a metal stand that stood like a large standard lamp at the side of the bed. The room was very bright, due to a strong white light that emanated from what looked like long white tubes built into the ceiling.

All along the walls, various strange-looking pieces of machinery hosted coloured buttons, levers, switches, wires and displays of differently coloured lights. Although the surroundings were very unfamiliar I felt quite relaxed and comfortable lying on the bed, until I tried to move my right arm and realised it was caught between the tubular bars at the back of my head. When I disentangled myself from the bed sheet to get a better look, I saw that a metal ring around my right wrist was attached to another ring around a bar at the top of the bed with both rings being joined by a chain – I was handcuffed to the bed.

My feeling of relaxation vanished and I was immediately gripped by a feeling of panic. I wrenched the wires from my chest and attempted to rise from the bed, causing the stand and the bag of yellow fluid to crash to the floor. This activity set off some sort of alarm and the sound of ringing bells and a buzzing noise brought a man and woman running into the room. The uniformed man made straight for my bed where he pressed down on my chest with one enormous hand and checked that the handcuffs hadn't been disturbed with the other. Satisfied I was secured to the bed, he stood back whilst the woman dealt with the fallen equipment and reunited me with my wiring and tubing.

'Take it easy, you're going to be okay,' she said, in a calm and reassuring tone. 'Now just relax and I'll get you hooked back up again.'

The calmness in her voice filtered through to me; I became less panicky and laid back down, whilst she busied herself reattaching the wires to my chest with the jelly. She made some adjustments to the box and the small blip reappeared following every beat of my heart. Although I figured she was a nurse, I'd never seen a nurse wearing the sort of uniform she was wearing. She wore long, white trousers of the type that I'd seen women tennis players wearing in old photographs and a white tunic-style jacket. In fact her clothes were more suited to a man than a woman.

The tall, stoutly-built man also wore a strange sort of uniform and, although I hadn't seen anything like it before, I was sure he was a policeman or perhaps a military man. He had all the mannerisms of someone with authority and when he appeared satisfied that the nurse was in control, he left the room. Just before he left, I heard him tell the nurse he would be outside and if I gave her any further trouble she was to call him immediately.

The nurse returned the stand to its original position, attached a new bag of the yellow fluid and pressed a pedal at the side of the bed, lifting me up into a sitting position.

'There you are,' she said, tidying the bed sheets. 'No damage done. Now what was all that about? Were you trying to get away?'

The question threw me. 'Away? Away from what?' I thought.

Suddenly the feeling of panic enveloped me again. I took a deep breath and made myself think about the situation. 'What was the last thing you remember?' I asked myself.

The question increased my feeling of dread when I found I couldn't remember any recent events or why I was in this place. Whether it was the fear or the injection the nurse had given me, I wasn't sure, but suddenly parts of my memory returned.

'I'm George Giles,' I told myself, 'I'm a twenty-seven year-old Londoner from Islington and a soldier in the British Army.' Having recalled these basic facts, I began to calm down but suddenly I became quite exhausted.

'Don't you dare go back to sleep on me!' I heard the nurse say. 'I'm just about to give you a shave and breakfast will be served soon.' At the mention of a shave I put my free hand to my face and felt a considerable growth of facial hair. 'This isn't me,' I thought. I made a point of shaving first thing every day. In fact, I abhorred beards and always mistrusted men who sported facial hair, whether they wore a full beard or a moustache. I always thought they had something to hide. Then the thought struck me.

'How long have I been here?' I was unaware that I'd asked the question out loud until the nurse responded.

'Just over a week,' she said. 'You've been here just over a week. Don't you remember being brought in?'

'Is this a hospital?' I asked her.

'Of course it is,' she said, with a note of surprise in her voice.

'Where am I and what am I doing here?' was my next question.

'You're on the fifth floor in intensive care,' she answered.

'I didn't mean what floor am I on!' I said irritably. 'What hospital am I in? What town is this?'

'It was probably the fall,' she said. 'You're probably a little bit amnesiac. There's no sign of a fracture so your memory will probably return in its own good time.'

'What fall?' I asked, becoming even more confused.

'You fell from the wall. Don't you remember? You were trying to escape.'

'Escape? Escape from what?' I shouted, frustrated.

'Broadmoor,' she replied. 'Broadmoor, the home for the criminally insane, as we used to call it. Now, just you relax! I'll be back in a moment.'

Before I had the opportunity to say anything else, she had gone and I lay back, dazed and confused, until she returned a few moments later carrying a tray holding some shaving equipment and a small mirror.

'What did you mean Broadmoor?' I asked. 'Before you left the room you said I came from Broadmoor. I've never been in Broadmoor in my life. There's been some grave mistake. You must be confusing me with someone else.'

'You'll have to discuss this with the doctors,' she said, as she lathered the shaving bowl. 'They'll be along to see you soon. Meanwhile, let's get you cleaned up, before I fetch you some breakfast. It's full English this morning, you'll enjoy that.'

Dismissing my protests with a smile, she pumped a lever at the side of the bed with her foot and this action raised me up a little higher into a sitting position. Then she produced a pair of clippers from a pocket on her tunic and began to clip away at my beard. When she was satisfied she'd removed the roughness she reached for the shaving brush and soap and lathered my face with a concoction that smelled more like a woman's perfume than shaving soap. Clearly she'd done

5

this before and handled the plastic razor with ease. When she finished shaving my face, she covered it with a hot towel for a few moments before drying it off.

'There,' she said. 'That's much better. Let me fetch you a mirror and you can see how nice and clean you look.' She leaned over and lifted the mirror from the tray at my bedside and held it in front of my face. 'What do you think?' she asked.

I looked into the mirror expectantly, but what I saw made me cry out in a state of alarm.

'That isn't me!' I yelled. 'That's not me! I'm George Giles! That's not George Giles!' I pushed the mirror out of her hand and tried to get up from the bed but the effort took too much out of me and I blacked out.

I don't know for how long I was unconscious. When I came round, I lay there thinking I was awakening from a terrible nightmare – until I realised I was in the same room and handcuffed to the same bed. Again, I had to fight off the fear that gripped my stomach, making me feel nauseous.

'There must be an explanation for this. There's bound to be!' I told myself, as I became aware of people around the bed who slowly began to come into focus. Another two men who I didn't recognise had joined the nurse and the guard. Both men were wearing identical white coats and the taller of the two spoke first,

'I'm Dr Wilson and this is my associate, Dr Watts. Do you know where you are?'

I didn't answer straight away, finding the question difficult. I was pretty sure I was in a hospital and the nurse had told me so, but I didn't know why. I had no sign of any physical injury or pain, apart from a blinding headache.

'Not exactly!' I said eventually. 'I believe I'm in a hospital but I don't know where and I don't know why. I expect you to provide me with an explanation.'

'Do you remember being admitted to hospital?' Dr Watts asked.

'No!' I said, somewhat irritably.

'You appear to be confused,' Dr Watts noted. 'Are you confused?' His patronising tone angered me and I found myself responding in quite an emotional way.

'Look,' I said. 'I don't know where I am! I don't know who brought me here! I don't know why I'm here! I don't know who the fuck you people are or what you want from me! When I look in the mirror I see a total stranger. Someone much older than me. Someone I've never seen before. Confused? You bet I'm fucking confused ...'

Before I could go on, Dr Wilson turned to the nurse and whispered something to her but I didn't quite catch what he said.

'The nurse will give you something,' he explained, seeing my curious expression. 'It will calm you down.'

'No!' I shouted. 'No more drugs. I want answers, not drugs! I want to know what's happening to me.'

Dr Wilson turned to the nurse and shook his head and she put the syringe back on a tray.

'Very well, Peter,' he said. 'But you'll have to try and control your emotions. We cannot have these outbursts. You must co-operate if we're to be able to help you. Please try to relax.'

His voice was calm and reassuring and I began to visibly quieten down.

'Perhaps a cup of tea would be better, nurse?' commented Dr Watts. 'What do you think?'

A cup of tea sounded like one of the most desirable things in the world at that moment and I nodded eagerly.

'Get me a cigarette as well, will you?' I shouted after her.

The request brought a puzzled look from both doctors but it was Dr Wilson who asked the question:

'When did you start smoking?'

His question perplexed me. I'd been a smoker since I was sixteen years-old and I'd never given up. Even during spells of bronchitis, chest infections, the flu and attacks of the common cold I never stopped. Nothing could stop me smoking – it was one of the few pleasures available during the war.

'I've always smoked,' I replied, and my answer seemed to satisfy them. For the next few minutes we sat in silence until the nurse returned with a tray holding a large pot of tea, some cups, little blue and white packets that contained milk and sugar, and a golden-coloured pack of twenty cigarettes. It wasn't a brand I'd seen before but I was happy to smoke anything at all so I grasped it eagerly when she offered it to me. It was covered in some sort of transparent material but eventually I got it opened and removed a cigarette. I put it into my mouth and the nurse bent over to light it with what looked like a metal cigarette lighter when I quickly pulled it out of my mouth.

'What's that?' I asked, turning the cigarette to show the end I'd put in my mouth.

She looked puzzled for a moment.

'It's a filter tip,' she said offering me a light. 'You put that end in your mouth and light the other,' she said, laughing.

Despite my suspicions I was so looking forward to a smoke that I went ahead and let her light me up. I took a couple of deep puffs and started coughing. I didn't know exactly what I was smoking and it tasted different from any other cigarette I'd had before. After a few more inhalations of the welcome smoke my lungs got used to it and I felt more at ease. I drank the tea and smoked in silence until the lull in the conversation was broken by Dr Wilson,

'I think we can remove the handcuffs for the moment, don't you?'

His question was aimed at the uniformed man who, after having his protests brushed aside by the doctors, unlocked the shackles. When I had both hands free, the two doctors, with the assistance of the nurse, helped me to my feet and into a chair by the window. The nurse went on to busy herself by changing the bed sheets and remaking the bed while the Uniform took up a position at the door. This was the first time I'd seen him side-on and I noticed he had what appeared to be a handgun in a holster attached to his belt. I use the word appeared because it was unlike any handgun I'd ever seen in my army career, and I'd seen a few.

The nurse finished making the bed and to her obvious displeasure Dr Wilson sat down on it opposite me, while his colleague sat on a chair next to mine. Over the next couple of minutes, Dr Wilson explained that I'd been brought into the hospital unconscious after suffering a blow to the head. Tests, he said, had shown no fractures of the skull or other physical problems. Apparently, I'd been unconscious until I came round that morning, but he expected I'd make a full recovery and the confusion I was presently suffering from would clear up.

I listened without interruption but nothing in what he said explained my current thoughts. I was a twenty-seven year-old man, but the mirror revealed a man in his late fifties who bore no resemblance to my mental picture of my own face. All my senses told me I was George Giles, but the mirror image looked nothing like him. Despite my inner terror I made a concerted effort to remain calm throughout the next few minutes.

'Do you remember what happened?' It was Dr Wilson again.

'I don't remember anything!' I said. 'Apart from the fact that I'm a twenty-seven year-old soldier serving with the British Army in Italy. I assume whoever brought me here would have explained this to you. I know nothing of Broadmoor.'

The doctor looked somewhat bemused. 'Why are you acting so surprised?' I asked him directly.

Dr Watt, who had clearly recovered his best bedside manner, elected to answer my question with some questions of his own.

'What kind of game are you trying to play, Peter?' he asked. 'You know you've been a patient at Broadmoor for the past ten years. Your name isn't George Giles. It's Peter Hunter. From 1985–1990, you murdered six women in and around the London area. That is six that we know about. You know there were others, don't you? You remember them, don't you? You remember your lawyer tried to get a plea of insanity accepted by the court but the judge threw it out and you were sent to prison for life? Of course, as many suspected, you later managed to convince the authorities that you really were insane and they shipped you to Broadmoor for the rest of your natural life. A man can't forget a thing like that. Can he, Peter? So what are you after? What's this yarn you're trying to spin about someone called George Giles?'

Almost every second he spoke I felt like interrupting him,

but I managed to contain myself and let him continue hoping to find out more about my situation.

'Ten days ago,' he was saying, 'you attacked a member of staff at Broadmoor and tried to escape over the wall. You almost made it, but slipped and fell, knocking yourself unconscious in the process. That's why you were brought here.'

'What does he mean, 1990?' I thought. 'What the hell is he talking about? If this guy Hunter has been in Broadmoor for ten years, that would mean this is the year 2000. It's only 1945. How could I have killed anyone almost fifty years into the future?'

Either I was in the middle of a nightmare or all the people in this room except me were mad … or perhaps I was the only mad one. I knew it wasn't a nightmare, so it was either them or me and I knew then I would have to get out of this place as soon as possible. I could not listen to any more of this talk about Peter Hunter and made my mind up that the only option was to get away from this place.

'I'm tired,' I said. 'Tired and confused. I don't feel up to answering any more questions or speaking about this just now. Can I be left alone? I need some sleep.'

Fortunately, this had the desired effect and both doctors rose from their sitting positions and assisted me back into my bed. Almost as soon as I lay down, I felt exhausted and just before I lapsed into sleep, I was aware of the Uniform putting the handcuffs back on my wrist.

Over the next couple of days I regained my strength. Physically, I was in good shape and had been throughout the war. My army training and fighting in Italy had seen to that. The doctors seemed happy to leave me alone and following a quick check-up each morning I was left in the care of the

11

nurse (but the Uniform was rarely far away). Bit by bit, I began to remember more and more about who I was. Despite the strange face that greeted me in the shaving mirror each morning, I was George Giles. Nothing or no one was going to convince me otherwise. I'd survived four years of war and I could survive this. After a few days the doctors began to interview me regularly and I was subjected to a number of tests – but they couldn't make me deviate from my story. I was allowed to exercise along the corridor of the hospital and slowly the drugs were withdrawn as I made good progress. On one of these walks with Dr Wilson and the Uniform not far behind, he suggested it was getting near the time when I should be discharged and taken back to Broadmoor. At that point, I decided to make my move as soon as possible. In bed that night, I tried to make sense of my position and lay motionless constructing my past piece by piece.

CHAPTER TWO

I was born in the London Borough of Islington, on 11th March 1918, in the family house at Linton Street, near the Regent's canal. When I was eight months old, we moved into a block of flats with three rooms and a scullery in Pickering Street, just off Essex Road. My dad was a soldier who was away most of the time and I shared the house with my mother, my two older brothers and my older sister. There was only one fire in the house to heat the three rooms and the dwelling was often damp and cold. I slept on a couch in my parents' room and an oil lamp that burned a foul-smelling liquid provided dim light. One morning I awoke covered in soot, as the lamp had been turned down too low and emitted a black smoke during the night. Everything in the room, including my mother, was covered in thick, black soot. The walls, ceiling and furniture had to be scoured clean and I recall my mother scrubbing the filthy bedclothes with Sunlight soap and Hudson's bleach whilst my father, who was home on leave, washed down the walls and ceilings.

The more I thought about my past, the clearer my memories became. I recalled little things that I thought I'd forgotten, like Christmas 1922 when I was given a Pip, Squeak and Wilfred annual and a train set; the cat meat shop next door to the pawn that sold second hand comics for a penny; and my first day at school.

My school was on Popham Road just a few minutes walk from Pickering Street. My mother took me along to begin my schooling on the first Monday after the Easter holiday in 1923. I was introduced to Miss Bone, a fair-haired lady, who showed me a cage full of pigeons that sat in the middle of the room.

She took hold of my hand and began to tell me all about the birds in a quiet, gentle voice and I was so engrossed that I never saw my mother leave the room. Years later, I realised the birds were simply a distraction to allow my mother to leave without me, before I could kick up a fuss. During the school holidays in July 1924, my mother took me to the Wembley Empire Exhibition. Every country in the Empire had an exhibit and I remember that Canada had a full-size statue of Edward the Prince of Wales made out of butter, housed in a glass refrigerator to stop it melting. New Zealand had models of hot geysers and there was a miniature railway that ran round the perimeter of the exhibition.

In 1926, my sister had a new baby daughter, so I became an uncle at the age of eight to my little niece, Mary. My grandmother died later that same year and I remembered I had a black china cat that she gave me, which I cherished for years until it was lost when we moved house.

Other things came to my mind, like my first holiday in 1929, arranged through the school. A group of pupils from Popham Road joined with others, as we left from St Pancras Station on a Friday morning, headed for Mountsorrel village in Leicestershire. When we arrived, we were boarded with the Crooks family in a house at number three, Boundary Road. The Crooks had a daughter Ivy, who was thirteen, and a son George, aged nine. As I recall the holiday was over all too quickly and I was soon back in London where things were pretty bad. My father had developed tuberculosis and couldn't work which meant we were always short of money. My brother Ted ran a public house called the Packington Arms, about ten minutes walk from the house, and he helped out as much as he could but we could rarely afford holidays, although I remember two in particular, both paid for by other people's kindness.

In the thirties, myself and some boys from the school,

who hadn't had a holiday that year, were given a day out by a millionaire, who opened his large country mansion known as 'Radlett' in Leicestershire to 'the poor boys of London.' We were given a hot meal when we arrived, along with some sweets and lemonade. For the rest of the day, we played football or explored the wooded area around the large house, where we climbed trees and made a swing using a large piece of rope we'd found tied to the back of an old tractor. The day went past too quickly and it was more than a year before I visited the countryside again. This time, a charity known as the Country Holiday Fund paid for some of us to have a vacation at the village of Ickleton in Cambridgeshire. These, and other memories, flooded my mind until I fell off to sleep.

My first thought the following morning was to take up where I'd left off, reflecting on my past. However, during the day, I was constantly drawn from my thoughts by the doctors probing and prodding in their attempts to make sense of what I was telling them. By late afternoon, I had convinced them that their constant questions had tired me out and I was finally left alone, apart from the guard, who was never far away but only spoke to me when he was issuing an order.

It seemed to me that most of what I remembered about my life was firsts. First Christmas, first day at school, first holiday and in keeping with this theme I thought about my first job after I left Popham Road School, at the start of the Easter holidays in 1932.

I was fourteen years-old and I got a job threading nuts in an engineering factory in Clerkenwell. I was too slow, and by the end of my first day I'd caught my fingers in the spindle of the machine so many times that I went looking for another job. A few days later I was offered a job as a 'clapper boy' with Gainsborough Film Studios in London – but my mother wouldn't let me take it as she didn't hold with actors and actresses or anyone connected with the stage or screen, so my job-hunt continued. A week or so later, I met my old headmaster, Mr Goodman, in the street.

'Hello, Giles, not working?' he had asked. I told him I wasn't and he advised me he had a friend who was a shareholder in Waterlow's, a printing firm in Moorgate, and he would get him to write me a letter of introduction. The meeting was indeed a fortunate coincidence as seven weeks after leaving school, I started as a copyholder with the firm. My wages were twelve and sixpence a week and I worked from eight in the morning until eight in the evening and from eight until noon on Saturdays. When I turned sixteen, I was offered an apprenticeship as a compositor but this involved a reduction in wages, so I found a job in another department that paid a little more than twelve and six a week. After I'd given my mother money for my keep, I usually had enough left to visit the cinema at least twice a week. I became a regular visitor to the Islington Empire and the Angel Cinema, where I saw films like My Old Dutch and Great Expectations. Inside a cinema was a great place to escape the poverty and misery of London in the thirties.

A day at the seaside was another means of escape and I remember sailing on a paddle steamer, the Laguna Belle, which plied her trade between the Tower of London and Clacton-on-Sea.

As these memories of my childhood and early manhood flooded back it suddenly came to me (and I couldn't understand why it had taken so long) that I was married! My wife's name was Olive: if anyone could sort this mess out it was her.

I met Olive in 1936 when she was working at Waterlow's and I discovered she lived in Ilford on Moorlake Road, a long thoroughfare off Ilford Lane. The realisation that I was married fired me to think even harder about my life. I began to remember all sorts of little things that were important at the time but which I'd forgotten years later: the journey on the number eleven tram from Moorgate to Highgate Village; visits to cinemas like the Finsbury Park Astoria, the Carlton, the Blue Hall Annexe and the Victoria in New North Road, as well as to the London Zoo. I remembered, despite the ever present threat of war, walks on Hampstead Heath and tea with Olive and her family on Sundays in 1939, the year I became twenty-one. At that age I qualified for a 'man's wage' of three pounds eleven shillings a week and felt I was quite well off, but a black cloud hung over the country.

In May 1939, the government announced that men aged twenty would be conscripted into the armed services. I'd turned twenty-one in March so I missed this conscription, but that didn't keep me out of the army for long. On Friday 1st September that year, I looked out the window from my workbench at Waterlow's into St Leonard Street when I heard the voice of a newsboy calling: 'Poland Invaded!'

Two days later, I sat round a battery wireless with my family and heard the Prime Minister Neville Chamberlain, tell the nation that Britain was at war with Germany. The following month I was passed fit for service by an army doctor and on 15th February, 1940, I became a soldier in the British Army earning fourteen shillings a week, quite a considerable drop in wages.

My basic army training took place at Crownhill Barracks in Plymouth, an infantry training depot, where we went under the name of the Duke of Wellington Regiment. In June 1940, my basic training was over and I was granted leave to get married before taking up my posting as one of three hundred other men who formed the 13th Battalion South Staffordshire Regiment. In December 1941, we would become the 104

L.A.A Regiment Royal Artillery, until I shipped overseas in 1943. Before that, I had various postings around England. At Holme-on-Sea on the Norfolk coast, my battalion built pill-boxes and laid mines along the east coast beaches. At Rye in Sussex, we assembled Bofors guns and did similar work at Chatham in Kent, Northiam and Minehead.

In 1942, my mother died and shortly after the funeral I sailed with my regiment from Liverpool, aboard the P & O liner Mooltan. We then joined a convoy at Greenock in Scotland and we headed out into the Atlantic to an unknown destination. Some days later, we sailed through the Bay of Biscay along the African coast to Sierra Leone and finally reached the Port of Durban in South Africa. We were there for about six days until we set sail again, this time headed for Bombay. There, we left the Mooltan and boarded a Polish minesweeper. This ship took us to the Iraq port of Basra where we headed inland to an army camp called Quetta, named after an earthquake in South America that killed thousands of people. After sometime at this camp, we were on the move again and our travels took us to Palestine, Syria and Egypt until we boarded another ship at Port Said and sailed to the Bay of Naples and Italy. By 1945, I was stationed in a small village near Rome that we'd liberated from the Nazis in 1944, but no matter how hard I tried I couldn't remember its name and I slowly drifted off to sleep with the image of a small Italian village etched in my brain and my mind filled with thoughts of making my escape from the hospital.

CHAPTER THREE

When I awoke the next morning, I knew I had to do it. If I didn't make a move, I had no idea what would become of me when I was returned to Broadmoor. I sensed that the guard was in his usual chair in the room so I made a groaning noise and made as if I was trying to pull myself up into a sitting position but slumped back down. This went on for a few moments before I attracted his attention. I heard him approach the bed and readied myself to muster as much energy as I could.

'Here, I'll give you a hand,' he said and bent over the bed, placing his hands around my shoulders to assist me up into a sitting position. When I judged his head was low enough I twisted my right arm that was still chained to the bedpost, thrust it forward and managed to loop the chain around his neck, between my arm and the post. I gave an almighty heave and he fell forward, face down on to the pillow. With my free arm I quickly grabbed his gun from its holster and placed it against his head.

'If you do as I say, you won't get hurt,' I said. He mumbled what I took to be consent and I slowly let him extricate himself from under my arm. He pulled himself to his feet and his eyes never left the gun that I held trained on his chest.

'Unlock the handcuffs!' I ordered. 'No sudden moves.'

He was not in the mood for heroics and did what I said without protest. When I was free, I rose from the bed and told him to stand against the wall, in a far corner of the room where I secured him with the handcuffs to what appeared to be a mains water pipe that ran down the side of the wall. I searched around the room and found some strong white adhesive tape with which I bound his legs and mouth. I suspected that it probably wouldn't take him too long to get free and raise the alarm, but I was satisfied that my efforts would hold him long enough for me to make my escape. However, I had another problem: I had no street clothes.

I looked around the room, but the only clothes I could see were those worn by the guard and a white coat that hung on a peg behind the door. I donned the coat and left the room and cautiously made my way along the corridor. I looked into every room along the passageway, until I came to one that held a single patient. He was clearly asleep and I spotted his clothes next to his bed. Within a few minutes, I emerged from the room dressed in a pair of navy blue trousers, a red jumper and a jacket made from some strange material that I'd never come across before. The shoes were also very odd. White-coloured with a thick-ridged sort of rubber sole, long white laces and the word 'Reebok' written along the sides. I'd never seen a pair of shoes anything like them before, but they felt comfortable enough when I got used to walking in them. I made for the stairwell at the end of the corridor and began to descend the long winding stairs. They seemed to go on forever and on each landing I stopped and looked through the small windows on the doors that led through to the passageway on each flight. Eventually I reached what looked to be the ground floor and I walked through the double doors, turned left past a reception desk and out through a revolving door into the fresh air. I was free! But what was I to do with my newfound freedom? Outside in the street, I turned to look up at the building I'd just left. It was the tallest structure I'd ever seen and I felt slightly dizzy until I took my eyes away. The rest of the scene outside was equally confusing as I entered this new world.

I started walking, quite quickly at first, until I'd put some distance between myself and the hospital. After a while, I slowed down and began to take in the scenes around me, as I strolled along through what should have been familiar London streets. About forty minutes later, I came across a small park that bordered a square next to a main road and three secondary roads. Inside the park, I sat on a bench facing the main road and tried to make sense of my situation. I was in London, I knew that. I'd passed many familiar landmarks before ending up here in the park, but it was a London that seemed to have changed a great deal.

The first thing that struck me was the bright blueness of the sky. The London I knew was always a drab and colourless place, with the fog and smog blocking out the sunlight most of the time, making the sky a dull, depressing grey. The roads and buildings looked very different too. Many of the buildings were taller than anything I'd seen in the city before. Cars and buses seemed to have changed beyond recognition. They looked like some of the futuristic machines I'd seen in comic books as a child and I couldn't believe the array of colours they came in, or the high speeds they achieved as they drove through the traffic lights, which themselves looked very different from what I remembered.

The jacket I was wearing seemed to have a large number of pockets and I fished around in them until I recovered a packet of cigarettes and what turned out to be a cigarette lighter. As I lit a cigarette, a woman, with a small child of about four years-old, sat down on the bench opposite mine. She fumbled around in a large canvas bag and produced what looked like a small, brightly coloured bag that I thought may be sweets. She opened it and gave it to the child who promptly went into a tantrum and threw the bag to the ground.

'Don't want them!' he bawled. 'Don't like cheese and onion!'

'Well you'll just have to do without then because there's nothing else. You can shout and scream all you want,' she said, dragging the child off in the direction of the park gate leaving the coloured packet on the ground.

I watched them leave the park and cross the road towards a shop. A few minutes later, they emerged from the doorway with the child in a much happier mood, having presumably managed to get his own way. As they made their way along the road my eyes alighted on the bag the child had thrown away. I bent down to pick it up and noticed it was made of some kind of silver paper. I put my hand inside, withdrew some of the contents and began to eat the crispy potatoes. They were not unpleasant, and within a few minutes I'd finished them when the thought struck me that this might be my last meal for sometime. I had no money, nowhere to sleep and no friends I could contact. If this were indeed the year 2000, all of my family and friends would likely be dead or at least very old. Again, I was struck by the same feeling of fear that I'd felt on and off since I first woke up in the hospital. I rose quickly from the bench and walked over to the small fountain that stood in the centre of the park where I cupped my hands under the falling water and drank copiously, washing the salty taste of the crisps from my mouth. After a few moments, I felt refreshed by the drink and the spray falling on my face. Suddenly, out of the corner of my eye, I saw the destination board on a large, red, double-decked bus. 'British Museum,' it read.

'That's it,' I thought. 'If there's anywhere I can find out what's happened over the last fifty odd years it's there in the museum.'

I set off through the park gate in the same direction as the bus, but the traffic was so slow-moving that within a couple of blocks I had overtaken it and stopped to get my bearings. After a moment or so I realised I wasn't that far from Great Russell

Street and set off along Bloomsbury Road. As I walked along, I noticed a group of people queuing at what appeared to be a machine of some kind built into a wall. Curiosity got the better of me, so I joined the back of the line-up to watch what was going on. As I drew nearer the front, I realised that the machine was dispensing what looked like money but the notes people were counting didn't look like any banknotes I'd seen before. I watched as they placed what looked like a small card into a slot on the wall, punched in some numbers after which the machine spat out banknotes. As the queue moved forward, I turned and headed off in the direction of the museum.

As I walked along, I thought about what I'd witnessed over the last hour or so and I was faced with the simple fact that no matter how crazy it was, I was in London in the year 2000. This being so, it followed logically that lots of things must have changed over the last fifty years. The bare fact was that I'd been missing for almost half a century, and of course, the world doesn't stand still. Within a few minutes I arrived outside the Museum and headed up the stairs, hoping that before the day ended I would come up with some answers.

Inside, the building was not as I remembered it, although I'd been there many times as a child and as a young adult. One of the staff was kind enough to furnish me with some writing materials when I lied to her, saying that I'd left my bag on the bus. She suggested I could use 'a computer' and I noticed she gave me a strange look when I said pen and paper would suffice. Armed with the writing materials, I found my way to the reading room and began my research by glancing through some newspapers. They all had the same date, 25th March 2000, which was over fifty years after the last thing I could remember. If that was the real date, and I was who I thought I was, I should be about eighty-two years-old. Although I believed I was George Giles, aged twenty seven, my reflection in a bookcase told me I was Peter Hunter: a fifty-five year-old psychopath. Panic began to grip me again, but I found the strength to resist it.

'Logic,' I told myself. 'There must be a logical position from which to start.' Of course, my whole position was illogical but somehow I convinced myself that there must be a rational explanation. 'Maybe this is what madness is like,' I thought. 'But I'm not mad. I'm confused! I'm scared! But I'm not mad. And what about the people I've spoken with since I came round in the hospital? They didn't appear to think I was mad. The librarian didn't treat me like a madman. She just gave me a strange look when I didn't seem to know what a computer was.'

After these thoughts I suddenly felt quite calm and told myself that if, for whatever reason, I'd been asleep for over half a century, many things must have changed. That was the position I decided to start from. I had to explore and understand this new world and with the library as my starting point, I began to search through a book index not exactly sure what I was looking for.

I'd been reading through the index intently for some minutes when I came across a book about the history of the 20th century. I noted its title and author and approached the librarian who told me to remain where I was while she fetched it for me. Within a few moments, she returned with a very large reference book.

'Here you are,' she said. 'If you're looking for something in particular the Internet may be better.'

Having no idea what the Internet was, I shook my head.

'No, I'm sure this will do,' I said. 'Thanks.'

'Well if there's anything else, I'll be at my desk.'

'Thanks,' I mumbled again, as she walked off.

I began by reading the introduction and noted that the book was a chronological history of major world events, starting from the year 1900, through to the beginning of the year 2000. Mostly, it contained newspaper clippings and photographs from around the world. Since 1945 was the last year I could remember, I decided that is where I would begin.

I turned the pages and read through the main news events of each month of that year. The war was the major story of every month and most of what was written I remembered as if it were yesterday, especially the part about the Italian Campaign, which my memory told me I'd been part of as a soldier, only a few months ago. I continued in this vein until I reached the month of November when I was shocked by what I read. There it was staring up at me from the page: the Japanese had surrendered after America had dropped an atomic bomb on two Japanese cities, Hiroshima and Nagasaki. I'd no recollection of this attack nor had I ever heard of an atomic bomb. There were rumours that the Americans were working on some sort of super bomb but rumours like that were rife on both sides. No matter how hard I tried I could not recall the Japanese bombings or any other happening beyond that month or the following months.

I moved on through the book month by month, year by year, and the most fascinating story was a report of the first moon landing in 1969. According to the book, twelve men had walked on the moon and that must be the most exclusive club ever, I thought. But other writings alleged that the moon landings never took place and the story of the 1969 landing and the others amounted to a huge hoax. The main 'evidence' centred around photographs allegedly taken on the moon, dodgy shadows and flags. But to stage such an enormous lie, I thought, would have involved hundreds, if not thousands of people, and I found it difficult to believe all of them would have kept their mouths shut for all those years.

As I continued reading, I learned that a great deal of change had taken place during the last fifty-odd years. In almost every walk of life, I read about new ideas and new technology. Apparently London had virtually been rebuilt after the Blitz. The old tramcar system had gone, replaced by cars, buses and trains. Millions of people owned things like colour televisions, computers, mobile phones and their own homes. Britain had lost most of her Empire and we had introduced a decimal currency and metric measurements. People used plastic cards to withdraw money from automatic banking machines in the street and they had an enormous range of food and drink to choose from. There were things available like home entertainment centres, foreign holidays, leisure and sports centres, theatres, film centres and much more. It seemed to me that anything a person desired was available as long as they had the money to pay for it (apparently many did so using things called credit cards). I read that in 1963, the President of the United States of America had been shot, but almost forty years later arguments about who actually pulled the trigger continued.

'What kind of world have we created?' I thought. It seemed that everything my generation had looked up to was being challenged: Parliament, the church, police, teachers, doctors – everyone with any authority. I was convinced I'd never be able to cope with this new humankind. Whatever had happened to me had occurred sometime before November 1945. Beyond that date, my memory was a blank. Briefly, I considered giving myself up to the police but the desire to remain free was too strong. Besides, I hadn't spent the last four years fighting to free others only to be enslaved myself. I had no idea what lay ahead, but I knew that the day was drawing to a close and

I'd have to find food and shelter before I considered my next move.

'We're closing,' I heard a voice say, bringing me out of my thoughts. It was the librarian. 'We're closing,' she repeated.

I shut the book, stuffed the notes I'd made into one of my jacket pockets and made for the exit. It was dark outside when I walked down the museum steps towards the main exit and when I reached the gate, I stopped suddenly and watched the scenes before me. People were walking in all directions, some of them stopping to look in the shop windows, others withdrawing money from cash machines, some were entering and leaving the pubs and restaurants, and others getting on and off buses. Although most of them were strangers to each other they all had one thing in common: they all knew who they were and where they were going. That was the difference between them and me.

I stood on the pavement, unable to decide whether I should turn left, right or cross over the road. I had no money, nowhere to stay and I could feel the hunger pangs grasping at my stomach. In the end, I turned right and started walking.

After a while, I found myself somewhere in the Regent's Park area where I spotted a small church on the other side of the road. I crossed over and went through the gate, up to the front door. I didn't know why, but I expected it to be open. On the left-hand side of the building there was a path between the church and the house. As I wandered up the path towards the rear of the church building, the one source of light came from an upstairs window of the house. I thought about knocking on the door to ask for help but I dismissed the idea and kept walking. At the back of the church, I entered a small walled garden and the light from the window reflected on what was a large greenhouse that ran the whole length of the back wall.

When I tried the greenhouse door it was locked, but with a bit of persuasion I managed to force it open.

Inside, it was warm, humid and very dark. Despite the darkness, I established that most of the greenhouse was occupied by tomato plants growing up to the roof. I pulled a few tomatoes from their branches and ate them greedily to stave off my hunger. When I was sated, I felt my way around, discovering a small gap between one of the long tables and the far corner of the greenhouse. I felt around under the tables and came across some material that smelled like old potato sacks. I stuffed as many of the sacks into one empty sack and made myself a pillow, huddled up in the corner and eventually fell off to sleep, wondering what the next day would bring.

CHAPTER FOUR

The heat from the sun radiating through the glass windows awoke me from my less than restful sleep. I pushed the makeshift pillow aside and was about to rise to my feet when I heard a movement above me, which made me cower back into my corner.

'Did you enjoy the tomatoes last night?' a soft, lilting, Irish voice asked. 'I wouldn't have thought they were quite ripe enough for eating, but I suppose if one is as hungry as you appeared to be, anything will suffice.'

At the sound of the voice, I froze, unable to speak.

'Come now, Mr Hunter,' the voice said. 'It must be most uncomfortable squeezed into that tight corner. Why don't you come out of there?'

He was right, it was uncomfortable, and having no other option I felt for the top of the table above me, took hold of it with both hands and hauled myself up on to my feet, expecting to be met by a number of policemen, but there was only one other person in the greenhouse: a priest.

He was quite a small man, about five feet six or seven, around sixty years of age and his long silver grey hair contrasted sharply with the blackness of his cassock. He continued silently watering the plants as if I wasn't there and when he finished he rested the watering can down on the floor and turned to look at me with the most piercing, bright blue eyes I'd ever seen.

'Well, Mr Hunter,' he said. 'You don't look like Britain's most wanted man, I must say. But that's how they are describing you on this morning's breakfast news. You look more like a man who could use a decent meal. Come with me and we'll have some breakfast. A man, even a wanted criminal, should always start the day on a full stomach.'

The idea of breakfast was more than appealing, so I followed him meekly out of the greenhouse and a few moments later we entered the manse. As we walked through the front door, I noticed the wide staircase on the right gave access to the upstairs parts of the house and on the left, a large open door led into a spacious sitting room.

'The kitchen's through here,' he said, leading me straight on past the staircase to the back of the house. 'My housekeeper's at the shops, but if you sit yourself down I'll make some bacon and eggs. I can just about manage that. Not much of a cook you see, but never had to be.'

I sat at the end of the kitchen table and watched him as he busied himself around the stove. Within a few minutes he had cooked some real eggs (not the powdered egg I was used to) and bacon in a large frying pan. He toasted and buttered some bread and made a large pot of tea, which he placed in the middle of the hardwood table, along with a salver of toast and two plates holding the warm food. Before I could begin to eat, he bowed his head and said a short prayer thanking God for what he and I were about to devour. Although I was ravenous, I managed to wait until he'd finished Grace before I tucked into the most delicious meal I'd eaten in days. For the next few minutes we sat eating and drinking in silence until the priest spoke.

'Well, Mr Hunter, did you enjoy that?' he asked, topping up my teacup with the warm, delicious beverage.

'I'm very grateful to you, Father,' I said. 'Very grateful. But my name isn't Hunter.'

'So what would your name be, then?' he asked. Before I could respond he continued, 'Are you a Catholic?'

'I am, Father,' I replied. 'But I haven't been to mass in a while.'

'When were you last at mass?'

I thought carefully about my answer before I spoke. 'It was during the War, Father, 1945.'

The piercing blue eyes stared me in the face.

'That was indeed a long time ago,' he said. 'Over fifty years. You don't look old enough or you must have been very young.'

'I was twenty-seven years-old in 1945, when I was stationed in Rome ... to me that was just a couple of months ago.'

He sipped slowly from his cup, his blue eyes betraying nothing.

'Is that a fact now? Rome, you say. Very interesting,' he commented. 'That would make you over eighty years-old and you don't look a day over fifty-five. Now, what kind of a story is this for a good Catholic boy to be telling a priest? Especially a priest who has just fed him. Sure, is that all the respect I get?'

'I have told you the truth, Father,' I replied. 'It would be easier to lie, but I am not Peter Hunter. My name is George Giles and when I awoke in hospital, in my mind the year was 1945. The last chapel I visited was the St John Lateran, in the San Giovanni district of Rome, and that was only a few months ago. I remember it clearly. There was a glass case before the altar that held a silver cross presented to the Chapel by a Spanish princess. There were thorns, said to have come from the crown of thorns placed on the head of Christ, and a piece of stone said to have been hewn from the boulder that was rolled before the tomb of Jesus. Before that, myself and others from my regiment were invited to meet the Pope at St Peter's after the liberation of Italy. The audience was held in the Sistine Chapel and I remember four Swiss Guards carried him into the Chapel on a bier. He mounted a raised platform where he delivered a welcome, saying how pleased he was to see so many English soldiers, first in English, then French and finally in Italian. That, too, was only a few months ago. Nothing anyone says can erase that memory from my mind. It was the greatest moment in my life.'

When it was clear to the priest that I had nothing more to add, he looked at me long and hard before he spoke. 'That is quite a tale,' he said. 'Quite a tale.'

Before he could say anything else, I rose from the table. I did not want to use force to get away, especially against this man whose kindness I'd found overwhelming, but I was prepared to do so if it became necessary.

'I'm very grateful for the food and shelter, Father,' I said. 'But I have to be on my way before the police arrive. Please don't try to stop me. I do not wish to hurt you.'

'The police?' the priest repeated, the tone of genuine surprise in his voice. 'Why for the life of me should the police be on their way here?'

'I assumed you must have called them?'

'I haven't called anyone. No one knows you're here. Why would I have called the police?'

His response stunned me as I'd taken it for granted that he would have alerted the authorities. But when I thought about it, it was over an hour since he'd discovered me in the greenhouse and he hadn't been out of my sight during the whole of that time. If he had called them before he came into the greenhouse, it surely wouldn't have taken them that long to arrive. After all, they were supposed to be looking for the most wanted man in Britain.

'I don't understand,' I said. 'I'm wanted by the police, you said so yourself. I'm the most wanted man in Britain according to the news, why would you let someone as dangerous as they say I am wander about, a free man?'

He rose from the table, filled a kettle with water from the sink and plugged it into the wall without uttering a word. When the kettle started hissing he lifted it and waved it before me.

'Some more tea?' he asked.

I nodded my agreement.

'I don't think I formally introduced myself,' he said, pouring the tea and laying the kettle down beside the sink. 'I'm Father Ignatius Cornelius Flaherty, Catholic Priest of this Parish, an alleged former member of the Irish Republican Army and in days gone by, a wanted man. Many years ago, you understand, things were very different then, of course. Back in the sixties, I mean. Very hard times. Very dangerous times.'

He held out his hand and grasped mine with a surprisingly strong handshake considering his advancing years and small stature.

'George Giles,' I responded.

'Well, George Giles,' he said, 'In the old days, back in Ireland, I met many a wanted man. Every one of them was described by the police as dangerous, including myself, but I believe the police and politicians tend to exaggerate in many cases and more often than not the truth is a stranger to them. Now let's take our tea into the study. Teresa, my housekeeper, doesn't allow me to smoke in the kitchen.'

I followed him into a sizeable room, with a high ceiling and a large bay window that overlooked a small flower garden and took up most of the wall. The wall to my left was completely covered by shelving that held hundreds of books and files. The one on the right housed a coal fire that burned brightly in the large fireplace and against the back wall a writing desk held a strange contraption that I later learned was a computer. In the middle of the room, a huge rosewood table sat surrounded by four comfortable-looking, dark wine coloured, leather chairs; the kind that usually adorned a gentlemen's club like the Carlton or New Cavendish.

'Please,' said Father Flaherty, offering me a cigarette from a silver case with a lighter attached to the side. 'Make yourself at home.'

I did as he bid me and sank into one of the leather chairs facing the fire.

As he watched the smoke spiral upwards from his cigarette he gave a small cough.

'So, you say your name is George Giles,' he said in a matter of fact way. 'The police say differently. They say you are Peter Hunter, who was detained at her Majesty's pleasure in Broadmoor asylum until recently …'

'Her Majesty?' I said.

'Queen Elizabeth,' he replied.

'When did King George die?' I asked. Again, here was something new I had to learn.

'About fifty years ago,' he said, 'don't you remember?'

Of course I didn't remember. I couldn't remember anything after 1945.

'If you're not Peter Hunter,' he said, 'as the newspapers and everyone else say you are, you bear a remarkable resemblance to him. In fact, you could be identical twins.'

'I cannot explain any of this, Father. In hospital, a nurse handed me a mirror and when I looked in it, I saw this man you see now. No matter how crazy this sounds, it is true.'

Before he could respond, our conversation was interrupted by a young woman entering the room. She was about thirty years-old, slim and a few inches taller than me. Her shoulder-length hair was a deep red colour, and she wore what looked like a man's suit with black shoes and a white blouse. She was carrying a brown briefcase that she laid on the writing desk before heading for the bay windows and throwing them open with a flourish.

'You've been smoking too much again, Father,' she said, 'it's like an opium den in here!'

'Now what would a nice, Catholic girl such as yourself know about opium dens?' he said, in a mocking but friendly tone.

Ignoring his remark, she turned from the window and looked at me with the most beautiful emerald green eyes.

'And who is this?' she asked, turning round to face the priest. 'I thought I'd left your diary clear for the day. Aren't you supposed to be playing golf with the Bishop about now? You didn't forget, did you?'

'There's been a change of plan,' he said, 'besides, I can never beat him. He cheats, you know.'

'Father Flaherty!' she said, like a mother about to scold a misbehaving child. 'You cannot go about saying things like that about the Bishop. You cannot accuse the Bishop of being a cheat!'

'But it's the truth,' the priest said. 'Of course, he makes out he's absent-minded but nobody believes that for a minute. He's only absent-minded when he takes an eight and cards a six. You can't win against him; he has the Pope on his side. In fact I'm sure it was the Pope who taught him how to cheat in the first place. They go back a long way together. Anyway, my game has been postponed until this afternoon so I have plenty of time. Now, to answer your question. This is Mr George Giles, an old friend.'

She walked towards me with her right arm extended and her green eyes bored into my brain.

'Pleased to meet you, Mr Hunter,' she said. 'He's such an old liar but I expect you'll have figured that out by now. Meanwhile, I have some business to attend to, so if you gentlemen will excuse me, I'll take my leave and if you must continue smoking, please leave the window open.'

At that point, I realised I was still holding her hand and I let it go and mumbled something unintelligible as she walked out of the room.

For the next couple of hours, I sat with the priest, smoking and drinking tea as I told him my story. He rarely interrupted, only doing so to clarify some point or other, as I relayed my account of my early days growing up in London, my family, friends, the War and my army buddies. It was difficult to figure out whether he believed any of what I said, but I felt better for being able to talk about it, although I still had no idea where my future lay.

'That's quite a tale', he said. 'Quite a tale.'

'It's the truth, Father,' I said. 'All of it is true.'

He took a long puff on his cigarette, watched the smoke rise into the air then looked directly at me.

'I don't doubt you believe you are telling the truth, but that, per se, does not make it so. The question must surely be why you believe it is 1945, when every piece of evidence shows we are in the year 2000. The War was a long time ago but, for some reason, to you it was only the other day. You claim you were born in 1918, but you don't look a day over fifty-five when in fact you should be over eighty years-old. The reports in the newspapers, about how you overpowered the guard at the hospital, don't suggest a man with the strength of an eighty year-old. In fact they suggest, as does your demeanour, that you are a very physically fit person.'

'I'm George Giles, Father.' I said. 'It doesn't matter what anyone else thinks. Your evidence is meaningless. I know who I am. I have no idea who Peter Hunter is.'

'Then perhaps it's time you found out,' he said. 'Since you don't appear to have anything else to do, or anywhere else to go, and half the country is looking for you, it may be prudent for you to stay here for a while. There are lots of little jobs that need doing around the place and you could earn your keep. Meanwhile, I'm sure Teresa will be willing to assist you in coming to terms with and understanding some of the changes that have happened to the world since you were last here. She has a thing called a computer. I have no idea how it works, but she seems able to find the answer to almost anything within a few minutes, including how much I spend on cigarettes and whisky every month.' He smiled at his own joke, rose from his chair and patted me on the shoulder.

'I know my story sounds incredible, Father, but it's absolutely true. Can you please believe me?'

He looked at me with a glint in his eyes. 'I suppose if I can believe in the Virgin birth and the resurrection of Christ without any difficulty, I can believe your story. Don't worry.

We'll help you through this crisis.'

When he closed the door behind him, I lit another cigarette from the box on the table and sat back in my chair. For the first time since I'd become conscious in the hospital, I felt someone believed me.

CHAPTER FIVE

Over the next few days, I rose early each morning and had breakfast, after which I tended the garden and did odd jobs around the house and church buildings. An assortment of people came and went throughout the day: postman, milkman, delivery drivers, members of the congregation and those down on their luck looking for some comfort or the price of another drink. I became quite adept at avoiding all visitors, fearing that one of them would recognise me as Peter Hunter, whose face was still appearing in the newspapers and on television, usually under headings such as 'Britain's Most Dangerous Man Still on the Loose'. To me, the headlines were patent nonsense. I wasn't a danger to anyone and if the police were closing in on me as the newspapers claimed, there was no sign of them from where I was situated.

After lunch each day, I continued with whatever jobs needed done and when Teresa left around four in the afternoon, I was permitted access to her computer. On my first evening at the church, she had taken me under her wing and shown me how to access the Internet and other basic functions of the machine. Within an hour or so I had become hooked, and every evening I spent hours finding out about this new world I had been catapulted into. I wasn't totally ignorant of communications systems. In the army I'd learned Morse code and was involved with radio communications, but this was something else. I began to understand the strange look the librarian at the British Museum had given me when I said I didn't want to use a computer and asked for some writing materials.

After many hours trawling through the Internet, I began to learn a lot about my missing years. Much of what I discovered depressed me. People seemed to have changed so much and although it may sound hypocritical, coming from someone who fought in a major war, the world itself seemed to have become a more violent place. It also appeared that those people for whom we were taught respect had lost the confidence of the young: the police, doctors, teachers and politicians among them. This wasn't a society I looked forward to living in, but the alternative of being confined in an insane institution was not an appealing prospect, either. It was a case of making a bad or worse decision. Either I could try to live as a free man, or surrender to my fate and give myself up. The instinct to be free was the greater, and so on my third night at the house I was again at the computer researching the life of Peter Hunter.

It was well after midnight when I shut the machine down and removed dozens of sheets of paper from the printer. Mostly the printouts were copies of newspaper articles about Peter Hunter or London's modern Jack the Ripper, as the newspapers had dubbed him. On analysis, his crimes bore little resemblance to those of the Ripper, who terrified the residents of the Whitechapel area in London during the 1880s. To me, the evidence said that Peter Hunter was simply a killer who murdered his victims for one simple reason: self-gratification. In the end he'd been caught, as is often the case, because he made an error of judgment when selecting his seventh intended victim. Unlike the Ripper, he did not confine his victims to women of a certain class. In fact, all of his victims were young women between the age of twenty and thirty, but apart from that they came from all sorts of backgrounds and did various jobs: a nurse, an accountant, a shop assistant, the owner of a flower shop, a hairdresser, and a computer consultant. It was his mistake in selecting a young woman who was in fact an off-duty policewoman and who also happened to be a self-defence expert. Although Hunter was much stronger physically than his slightly built victim, she outmanoeuvred him and disabled him with a pepper spray, giving her time to set off a personal alarm. Within minutes of the attack, he was arrested and was later found guilty of six counts of murder. At his trial, his defence team tried to get the prosecution to accept a plea of guilty to manslaughter on the grounds of diminished responsibility, but the judge rejected the move and put the matter before a jury. In essence the trial was a formality. The evidence was overwhelming and the jury had little difficulty in returning a verdict of guilty on all counts. Psychiatric evidence concluded that Hunter was a paranoid schizophrenic, but he was sentenced to life imprisonment with a recommendation that he serve at least thirty years.

In my day, he would have been executed within a fortnight but another thing I'd learned was that Britain had scrapped the death penalty in the sixties. As it turned out, Hunter had managed to convince the authorities that he was insane and he was moved to Broadmoor a few months after his trial. According to the reports, Hunter had spent most of his time in Broadmoor in solitary confinement after being attacked by other inmates until his escape – which was reported in great detail. None of what I read made any sense to me. If I was indeed Hunter, surely I would have some recollection of these events? But I only had memories of my life as George Giles.

With these thoughts running through my head, I lit another cigarette and glanced at the clock on the mantelpiece above the fire: It was almost four o'clock. Over the last few hours I must have read hundreds of words about the man I was supposed to be. I may have his face, I thought, but that was as much as we had in common. I'd been trained to kill in the army but fortunately, I was never called upon to do so. By the time I'd finished my training and shipped abroad, the Germans were on the run and my regiment had the habit of arriving in towns and villages days after they'd left (and I remembered often thanking God many times that we had done so). Killing in time of war was one thing, but taking someone's life for self-gratification or financial gain, in my view, was abhorrent. I read that the first known assault by Hunter was on a July evening in 1974, when he attacked a twenty-six year-old woman who was walking home alone, striking her unconscious with a hammer and slashing her with a knife. Fortunately for the woman, he was disturbed by a neighbour and fled before killing her. The next month Hunter attacked a twenty-eight year-old woman, but was again disturbed and left her alive but badly injured.

On 30th October, that same year, he committed his first murder that the police came to know about. His victim, a thirty year-old mother of three, was struck by a hammer before he stabbed her thirteen times. He did not kill again until the following year. In January 1975, he stabbed a twenty year-old woman over fifty times. In February, another woman was lucky to escape with her life when he attacked her, but the following month he claimed his third victim. Again, he struck her with a hammer and repeatedly stabbed her although the post-mortem revealed she was already dead when the stabbing occurred. Two months later he killed a twenty-eight year-old prostitute in her London flat where police found a boot print on the bedclothes. And two months after that killing, a sixteen year-old girl became his fifth victim. Finally, his last victim before he was caught was another young London prostitute, again murdered in her own flat.

I finished my cigarette and was just drifting off to sleep, when I suddenly remembered something I'd read earlier. This brought me wide-awake and I lifted the papers from the floor and leafed through them until I found the piece. It was from the London Evening Standard, written by a journalist called David McIntosh. From the first murder, McIntosh had followed the investigation all the way through until arrest, trial and sentence. He'd been granted permission to accompany the scene of crime officers and the detectives investigating the case. After the trial, McIntosh predicted that Hunter would manage to convince the authorities that he was mentally ill, in order to be moved from prison to a hospital. McIntosh had interviewed him a number of times from his new home in Broadmoor and eventually he wrote a book about the case. In the book, entitled *Evil Within*, McIntosh had argued that society would inevitably have to accept that there are some people in the world who are simply evil. They are not mentally ill or suffering from any other medical aberration. They are simply bad people with no conscience and no remorse for their actions. Hunter, according to McIntosh, was such a person regardless of what his psychiatrists said, and the evidence of Hunter's crimes suggested the journalist was right. It became apparent that David McIntosh was probably the one person in the world who knew what made Hunter tick. If I was to make any sense of what was happening to me, I felt that this journalist was the key, and somehow or other I had to make contact with him. Tiredness began to overcome me and I slowly dropped the papers to the floor and fell asleep with a feeling that I hadn't had for sometime: hope.

CHAPTER SIX

When I arrived downstairs the next morning, I heard voices coming from the study. Father Flaherty was in conversation with another man and for a moment I was tempted to listen behind the door, but I overcame the urge and went into the kitchen as quietly as I could.

'Is that you, George?' Father Flaherty called after me. 'Come into the study when you've had your breakfast, there's someone I'd like you to meet.'

The last thing I wanted to do was meet anyone. I figured the more people I met, the more chance I had of being arrested, but I could not ignore his request without causing his guest to become suspicious.

'Good morning, Father,' I said, as I entered the room some ten minutes later. 'I'm sorry I appear to have overslept, I was up very late.'

'Have you had breakfast?' he asked. 'A man should not ...'

' ...Start the day on an empty stomach.' I finished his sentence. 'I've had some tea. I'll eat later,' I said.

'Quite, quite! There's someone I'd like you to meet,' he turned to the man sitting beside him.

'This is ... well let's just say for now, he's a friend.'

The man rose from his chair and shook my hand. He was quite tall: about six feet, slim build, wearing a navy blue suit with a pale blue shirt and a dark blue tie. He had short, well-groomed, brown hair with a little grey here and there and I thought I detected a hint of an East London accent. I figured he was between forty or fifty years-old.

'Pleased to meet you,' he said, clasping my outstretched hand. 'Names are not important at this stage.'

When the three of us were seated there was an awkward silence for a few moments until Father Flaherty spoke.

'I don't want you to worry about this, George, but I've been speaking with our friend here about your case. Your secrets are safe with him, I assure you. Trust me! Now, as I'm familiar with your story, I'll leave you two gentlemen to get to know each other. I'll arrange for some tea.'

With that he left the room and again there was an awkward silence, which I decided to break.

'What would you like to know?' I asked. 'What can I tell you?'

'Everything you know about Peter Hunter may be a good place to start,' he said.

'All I know about Hunter is what I was told in the hospital and what I've read over the past couple of days. Chiefly stuff from newspaper articles and reviews of a book by a chap called McIntosh. Nothing more.'

'So you deny you are him, is that it?'

His question irritated me. 'I'm George Giles,' I said curtly. 'I may be confused about what year I'm living in but I know who I am. I may look like this man. My face may have changed but inside, in my soul, I am George Giles. No one else.'

'You look remarkably like Peter Hunter, despite the growth of beard you have there,' he said. 'Then, of course, there's the DNA evidence, eyewitnesses, nurses and doctors at the hospital, the staff at Broadmoor, newspaper photographs and television pictures. All of them reveal you are Peter Hunter –

convicted killer. Quite compelling evidence, don't you think?'

I knew what he was saying was technically correct and I couldn't think of a response that would make sense, but I felt I needed to reply so I blurted out: 'It's just circumstantial!'

'Who finds the heifer dead?'

'What?' I asked. 'Sorry, I don't understand what you mean.'

'Shakespeare, *Henry VI*. Don't you remember? The prosecutor used it to great effect in your trial. "Who finds the heifer dead, and bleeding fresh, and sees fast by a butcher with an axe, but will suspect 'twas he that made the slaughter?" You don't remember?'

I was becoming irritable again. 'I wasn't at any bloody trial!' I shouted, 'and perhaps to my eternal shame, being an Englishman, I know nothing about Shakespeare apart from the little smatterings I learned at school, and I've forgotten most of them by now. I'm not a literary person. True crime, detective novels, books on sport, that's about my limit.'

'So! No poetry. No Blake, Shelly, Oscar Wilde?'

I laughed. 'Where I come from poetry is for sissies.'

He eyed me carefully before he spoke: 'how about music art, drama, film, literature, ballet, that sort of thing?'

'I'm afraid I know as much about that as I do about canal navigation. Not my cup of tea. My tastes are much simpler. I've never understood the point of this art business. So much pretentious rubbish, if you ask me. Sorry, but I like what I like. Besides I don't know what any of this has to do with my present situation, which I'm more concerned about. Father Flaherty seems to think you'll be able to help but I can't see what my artistic tastes or lack of intellectual pursuits have to do with anything.'

Again he eyed me very carefully before he responded.

'Sometimes,' he said, 'sometimes, you can learn a lot about a person through their activities and intellectual pursuits, as you put it. The books and poetry they read, the music they listen to. Hitler was a lover of Wagner, for example. Many say his music is anti-Semitic. It doesn't follow, of course, that all people who love Wagner are by definition anti-Semitic, but it makes you think. Don't you agree?'

I certainly didn't agree, and frankly didn't care much for his intellectual ranting as I saw it and for the next twenty minutes or so I became more and more irritated by his constant, and what I deemed to be banal and meaningless, questions. Our conversation came to an abrupt end when I blurted out somewhat angrily in response to another of his questions.

'Listen, I awoke in a hospital bed believing my name was George Giles and it was the year 1945. Nothing, I mean nothing, is going to change my mind as to who I am. I have to accept that it is not 1945, on the evidence before me. So, I've lost fifty-five years of my life, but I'm still who I say I am. Whether I like Beethoven over Brahms isn't going to make a blind bit of difference to that.'

I would have continued in this vein but he rose from his chair, went over to the door and opened it.

'Are you there, Father?' he called out into the hallway, before returning to his seat. At the exact moment he did so, Father Flaherty came into the room, closing the door behind him. He lowered himself slowly into his chair, reached for the cigarette box on the table, took out a cigarette, lit it and spoke through the smoke.

'Well, gentlemen!' he said. 'I hope you had a fruitful conversation.'

It had been far from fruitful in my view and I simply shrugged.

'George!' the priest said, 'I'd like to introduce you to our friend. Meet David McIntosh.'

'So that was it,' I thought, 'Father Flaherty has beaten me to the punch. He'd figured the same thing: that David McIntosh was the key. I'd just been through some sort of test.'

Before I could say anything, Father Flaherty continued,

'I don't think there's anyone in the world who knows and understands Peter Hunter better than David. He's interviewed Hunter more times than I can remember. If you were indeed him, you won't have fooled David. I can assure you of that.'

Again I tried to say something, but was interrupted by David, who held out his hand.

'I'm pleased to meet you, George,' he said.

The fact that he addressed me as George brought a feeling of hope and I instantly felt angry with myself for my earlier rudeness.

'I'm very pleased to meet you,' I blurted out. 'I've been wondering how I could contact you, but Father Flaherty has obviously outwitted me on this one.'

David laughed aloud at my remark.

'You're not the first person this wily old codger has outwitted George, and you won't be the last. In fact there's quite a long list of victims, myself included. The Father and I go back a long time. Indeed, you could say we're old friends.'

Father Flaherty took another long drag on his cigarette.

'So, David,' he said. 'What's the verdict on our new friend here?'

My excitement rose at the question and I felt a fluttering in my stomach. David looked at me before turning to the priest.

'If you'll excuse my language, Father,' he replied. 'I don't know what the hell is going on here, but this man is not Peter Hunter – of that I'm convinced.'

At this statement my anxiety all but disappeared and I felt a well of emotion. I moved to speak, but the words never came and David raised his hand to indicate I should remain silent.

'He may look like Hunter, in fact his DNA may match that of Hunter, but I really don't give a shit. Sorry, Father.' The Priest waved his apology aside and David continued:

'I spoke with Hunter many times. The most memorable thing about him was his eyes. They were dead. They never betrayed any emotion, even when he spoke about the killings he was responsible for. He really believed he was the most powerful person on Earth. Everything about him was cold and calculated. He had the IQ of a genius, and the only thing that was larger than his IQ was his ego. He couldn't help showing off. He'd quote Shakespeare, Burns, Blake, Wilde at the drop of a hat. If I misquoted a literary figure, as all of us do in our desire to impress or support a point, he'd immediately correct me and he was always right. He demanded editorial rights to the book I wrote about him, and to be honest he made a far better job of editing it than my editor could have done. I don't know who George here really is, but he's not Peter Hunter. Every part of my logic tells me that he must be: but my heart, soul and experience tell me something totally different. I'm confused beyond comprehension and can only say that no matter how crazy it sounds, there is something going on here that's beyond the normal.'

Whilst David was speaking, I sat listening intently and watched Father Flaherty's reactions but he gave little away.

Now he spoke, addressing his remarks to David.

'If it's beyond the normal, are you saying it's paranormal? Is that what you're saying?'

David's response was not what I expected.

'Father,' he said, 'you know I don't hold with theories of ghosts, spirits, aliens or any of that other mumbo jumbo that you guys give out.'

Father Flaherty laughed. 'That's because you're a fucking heathen.'

Noticing that I was quite shocked by his response, the priest apologised.

'Excuse my language, George,' he said, 'but there are some people in the world who are simply heathens and there's nothing that can be done for them. But David, well, David is different. He's intelligent enough to understand but simply won't make the effort. He has no faith, you see. He's obsessed with proving everything to the nth degree. He has not yet begun to try and understand the difference between a believer and a non-believer. He wants proof all the time and there are more things in Heaven and Earth that can't be proven than there are things that can be. But having said that, he's really quite an agreeable person and one day he'll come round to my way of thinking, of that I'm sure. It may be a bigger conversion than St Paul on the road to Damascus, but it will happen.'

David simply laughed at the Father's remarks and when he did so I was struck by the real friendship and respect these two men clearly held for each other. One a believer and the other a non-believer; but both of them comfortable with their friendship, their tolerance of each other's opinions and their honest acceptance of the other's right to hold a different viewpoint. It was Father Flaherty who pulled me from my thoughts.

'So, where do we go from here?' he asked. His question could have been directed to either of us, but it was David who replied.

'We have to get you out of London, George,' he said. 'We need time to get to the bottom of this. If they catch you, they'll send you back to Broadmoor. After a couple of days, the media feeding frenzy will die down – no one will give a shit about you and the wider world will forget you exist.'

Things were beginning to move a little too fast for me and my mind raced with questions. I had no money, no job, and no place could I call home. Not only that, but I had no identity other than that of Peter Hunter, a psychopathic killer. As if he'd read my mind, Father Flaherty spoke.

'Setting you up with a new identity will be easy enough. The most important thing just now is getting you out of London,' he said.

I thought for a moment before saying anything. When I did, I told these two new friends, the only friends I had in the world, that I was afraid that they could find themselves in serious trouble with the authorities if they were caught assisting me. Perhaps it would be better if I just went on my way and let whatever would happen, happen.

'Don't be stupid,' Father Flaherty said, 'you'd be caught in a matter of hours. Besides, the church has been a place of sanctuary for centuries. It has a long history of providing comfort and support to the prosecuted and afflicted. The law of sanctuary may have changed, but the principle remains the same. In any case it's unlikely they'd find a judge who'd send a God-fearing priest to prison for refusing to reveal something that has the protection of the confessional.'

'I don't recall having been to confession recently, Father,' I said.

He laughed at my remark and I swear his speech became more Irish than before.

'Well now,' he said. 'The rules on what constitutes an actual confession are quite complicated. Perhaps just a little bit too complicated for the police to understand. In fact, you could probably say that another priest or an Archbishop can only really understand them. A lot is in the interpretation, you see. As for David here, while he doesn't have the protection of such complicated rules as those of the church, there is also reluctance on the part of the government to jail journalists. It's not really a good idea in the long-term. Checks and balances, democracy, freedom of the press – all that sort of baloney. So if I were you, I wouldn't worry too much about what may happen to us. It's also a fact that the police are looking for Peter Hunter and since you're not him, we'll have done nothing wrong.'

It was a simple remark, but it brought me such a feeling of comfort to know that I was believed. For the next few hours we sat and discussed a strategy to get me out of London.

CHAPTER SEVEN

The next morning after breakfast, David drove us to Euston Station. I felt a little uncomfortable dressed in a priest's garb, but Father Flaherty assured me that I looked fine and that no one would give a second look to one priest seeing another off on a train. He'd also issued me with some stock phrases I could use in the event I was asked for help by any troubled fellow traveller on the journey.

'Let them talk through their troubles,' he said. 'Quite often that's all they need to make them feel better. A problem shared is a problem halved, as the saying goes. Provide them with a listening ear and remind them that God acts in mysterious ways, his wonders to perform.'

He was right about talking a problem over with someone else. I could testify to this benefit personally, as after speaking with him and David I'd managed to convince myself that no matter how crazy my situation was, things would work out in the end.

It was around ten-thirty when we entered the station, which to me had changed beyond recognition. It was nothing like I remembered and now looked more like a shopping centre than a railway station, with shops and stalls on every wall and available space in the forecourt selling everything from bananas to car insurance. My memory was of steam trains and a small station shop that sold newspapers, cigarettes and sweets.

David had said his goodbyes in the car and I waited outside whilst Father Flaherty went to buy me a ticket. When he returned, we walked down the ramp to the platform and he handed me the ticket and an envelope.

'There's some money in there, along with a bank card and instructions for its use as well as directions to David's flat in Glasgow. Remember to keep the mobile phone switched on and don't forget to charge the battery regularly. The journey takes about seven hours so you've plenty of time to familiarise yourself with all this modern technology. I'll be in touch. Ah here we are, Coach D.'

We stepped aboard the train and not unsurprisingly it was unlike any other I'd ever seen. In my day, trains had individual carriages and you were confined within that space for the whole of the journey. A leather strap with holes allowed you to open and shut the window but you were usually blackened by the smoke coming from the engine if you kept it open or some other passenger would complain about a draught. If it was kept closed, the heat was usually stifling and on most journeys there would be much debate about whether it was too warm or whether there was too much of a breeze. The old joke was that if you opened the window yourself it was fresh air, but when someone else opened it, it was a draught. Also, there was no question of walking up and down the length of the train. Some coaches had an aisle that allowed you to move from one part of the train to another, but I think they were only employed on long journeys or for first class passengers. When we entered Coach D, most of the seats were occupied or held a ticket on top signifying that they were booked in advance. There were two seats at the rear end of the coach next to the door, leading into the next coach that lay empty. I headed for them, followed by Father Flaherty and made myself comfortable on the seat next to the window, placing my small bag on the seat beside me. Father Flaherty stood in the aisle, his right hand resting on the luggage shelf above the seats.

'There is an end to every horror,' he said. 'This journey

may signal the end to yours. Have faith.'

He removed his hand from the shelf.

'Good luck,' he said, patting me on the shoulder, then suddenly he was gone.

For a minute or so, I sat more than a little confused and mostly unaware of the actions taking place in front of me. When I eventually looked up, people were storing bags on the overhead shelves, speaking on their mobile phones, removing clothes, checking seat numbers, arguing about who was to sit where, eating, and drinking, and asking each other a variety of questions about timetables, stations, stops, arrival times, toilet facilities and a whole host of other trivia. Travelling in the twenty-first century seemed to be a very complicated process, I thought. In my day you boarded the train, sat down, selected a book, magazine or a newspaper to read or went to sleep, and that was that until your journey terminated. Sleep, I considered, was perhaps the best thing I could do but my mind was too full of unanswered questions for this to be a realistic proposition. As people hovered about, I watched their faces and began to wonder if anyone would recognise me and raise the alarm. If they did, I asked myself what I would do. Would I run for it and risk being shot by the police? Surrender and spend the rest of my life in a mental institution? In truth I didn't know the answer. Rather than think about the future, I began to evaluate the present. I was on a train to Glasgow, to a flat owned by David McIntosh, under instructions to remain there until I was contacted. Courtesy of his newspaper I had some money, a mobile telephone and a bank card that I could use in emergencies in one of the cash machines I'd first seen when I escaped from the hospital. I removed the mobile phone from my pocket and spent the next twenty minutes or so checking that I understood how to operate it. I sent myself a few text messages and was quite proud when they actually arrived and

I could access them. It was much simpler than I'd first thought and I felt confident enough to put it back into my pocket, happy in the knowledge that I'd be able to make a call or answer one when necessary. A sudden jerk of the train pulled me from my daydreams and when I looked out the window, we were on the move. Very slowly at first, until the train began to gather speed. Feeling relieved we were on our way, I lit a cigarette and began to relax. I'd gotten over the first hurdle and was on my way out of London. I lay back, closed my eyes and began to think again about the last time I had travelled north on my way from London to Liverpool, in January 1943. I felt sure if there was an answer to my dilemma it lay overseas.

CHAPTER EIGHT

On the 11th of March 1943, my twenty-fifth birthday, we crossed the equator. A few days later we were in the city of Bombay. After we docked, we were allowed to go ashore, but only if we wore our dreaded pith helmets. As we passed a shop window, I couldn't resist looking at my reflection to see how I looked with this monstrous object perched on top of my head. Suddenly, a voice from behind barked, 'Don't you salute officers?'

I turned my head to be confronted by an officious captain and as I did so only my head moved and the helmet, which was far too big for my head, remained static and so was now back to front. I saluted in any case, but if he had a sense of humour he must have laughed later on. Unfortunately, Bombay was not a city that provided much by way of laughter and despite the pamphlets, we were not prepared for what we saw.

There were old men with no legs being pulled through the streets on four-wheeled trolleys by young children, begging as they went, and there was a terrible stench and billions of flies. It was something of a relief when we were told we were due to sail, but we were to say goodbye to the Mooltan that had brought us all the way from Liverpool to India. Our new ship was a Polish minesweeper, the name of which no one, apart from the Poles, could spell or pronounce. It was a much smaller ship, but it was comfortable enough and a few days later we sailed through the Persian Gulf and along past a ridge of seemingly endless mountains until we reached the port of Basra, where we disembarked. Our long voyage across the ocean was complete and we'd never come face-to-face with the enemy.

We were billeted at a camp called Quetta and after a day or so we settled down to our new environment. As it transpired, we were only in Baghdad for a couple of weeks whilst we acclimatised and soon we were headed for other parts. Our destination was a plateau some sixty miles from Baghdad and I climbed into the back of an old South African truck, which had seen better days, and sat armed with a Thompson machine gun, watching our man-made sandstorm as we sped through the desert.

Everything went well enough for the first fifty miles, but driving thorough an Arab village the engine suddenly stopped. Soon we were surrounded by a horde of children from the village all wanting to touch the truck. I took a loaded magazine from my pouch and quietly slipped it into my gun, and in a show of bravado waved it towards the crowd with a few well-chosen words of Arabic and English, but the children were unimpressed. Thankfully, before anything untoward happened, a Royal Artillery column appeared to give us a tow and we went on our way, leaving the village behind without incident.

We reached our encampment as night fell and in the gloom I saw a light from one of the tents. I walked over and pulled open the flap.

'Good evening, sir!' I said, scaring the living daylights out of two officers who were sitting inside enjoying gin and tonics.

When daylight came we took stock of our surroundings and most of what we saw was sand and more sand. There were a few empty tents, which would later be occupied by the main body of troops, and a few brick buildings, that would serve as a storehouse and cookhouse. After the main body arrived we settled down to a normal routine, but the heat was practically unbearable and we could not touch our Bofors gun because the metal was so hot. Fortunately, a nearby expanse of water that flowed from the River Tigris provided a means of keeping cool.

Late one night a storm blew up, causing the tent to sway violently from side to side. I climbed out of my makeshift bed on top of ammunition boxes and grabbed the tent pole. Suddenly, above the sound of the wind, I heard the most blood-curdling howl that froze my blood. Outside, there was a pack of wild dogs that had smelled the meat from the cookhouse nearby. Eventually the wind died down and someone chased off the dogs.

Six weeks later, we were on the move and at the end of a week's travel entered into the Jordan Valley and a few days later we crossed through enormous olive groves into Palestine.

The following morning we were off again, but this time only a few miles along the coast to Beirut where we stopped at a place called Kiryat Haim, a Hebrew settlement beside the Mediterranean. Our camp consisted of a few huts: baths, showers, latrines and a cookhouse. Blessed luxury compared to the horrors of Iraq.

The main railway line to Cairo ran alongside the camp which was ringed by barbed wire, but that didn't stop a delegation of Jews going to our officer for help when dried grass near their village caught fire. They accused an Arab of throwing a lit torch from a passing train which could very well have been true but the train was gone and there was little we could do about it. However, we could assist with putting the fire out so we clambered over the wire carrying spades.

The next day, a captain was required at another unit some miles away and I was assigned as his armed escort. After a few miles, we passed through a small village with a sign in both Arabic and English: Nazareth. After the captain's meeting was over I had the opportunity to stand by the Sea of Galilee in a moment of very quiet contemplation, as the waters lapped over my army boots. Across the lake, the officer pointed out the site of the Temple of Capernaum where Jesus had preached all those years ago.

A few weeks later, we were on the move again for a short stay in Lebanon, before arriving back in Palestine where we set up a camp at St Jean. We spent Christmas 1943 at St Jean and then shortly afterwards moved on to Beirut and then Tripoli, where we occupied the two upper floors of a large modern block of flats. A few months earlier, the Italian fleet had surrendered and it was clear that the Allies were winning the war, and our days in Syria, Lebanon and Palestine were numbered. We heard that our next stop was to be the town of Tel-el-Kebir in Egypt, where there was a large Eighth Army vehicle compound; a military hospital, ammunition dump and a military garrison surrounded by barbed wire and mines and of course, sand. After a short stay at Tel-el-Kebir, we left early one morning for seven days leave in Cairo. When we arrived in the city we reported to the military police, who informed us we would be staying at Marnia Hotel across the road from the famous Shepheard's Hotel that was reserved for officers. When our leave was over, we returned to the barracks and some days later we were told we had gone as far east as we could and now we were heading west.

On our way to Port Said we passed a POW camp that housed mostly Germans of the elite Africa Corps, and despite the fact that they were prisoners of war, they looked a most formidable body of men. Speculation of where we were headed was rife, with some saying we were going back to England and others that we were to become part of some European invasion, but after a couple of days the convoy split up, with part of it headed for Gibraltar whilst the rest, including my ship, sailed along the Italian coast and entered the Bay of Naples. Sadly, on first sight it was not as beautiful a view as the poets had described it over the years. Sunken ships protruded from the water all along the bay, courtesy mainly of our own RAF and as we marched through the city the signs of war were everywhere. Broken buildings, burned-out vehicles, beggars in the streets and in one part of the city a graveyard had been hit and its contents scattered all around – it was a most grisly sight.

That night we slept in the open and in the morning we prepared to move off. For most of the day, we sat around doing nothing until later that evening we boarded American-style railway wagons with large wooden sliding doors. It was a warm evening and slowly we left Naples behind until some miles later we saw the sky glow a most brilliant red colour, but it wasn't the evening sun: Vesuvius was erupting. It was an awe-inspiring sight!

Slowly, we made our way through the night with a series of stops and starts until morning came and the train came to a halt. As daylight came in through the carriage windows, it brought with it pangs of hunger and thirst and we went in search of some food. At the end of the carriage we saw smoke begin to appear and on investigation we found a sergeant and three soldiers had lit a fire on the metal plate between the coaches on which they were boiling water to make tea. This was happening along the length of the train and as the carriages filled up with smoke it must have looked from the outside as if the whole train was on fire.

'Haven't you anything to eat?' the sergeant asked, as he saw us looking longingly at the biscuits he was sharing out with his men.

'No!' I replied pathetically, at which he kindly arranged for us to have some biscuits and tea – the best I've ever tasted. In conversation, we found out the train was heading east for

Brindisi. In our new home, we passed the time drilling and attending training sessions on mines. We found out our anti-aircraft guns on the way from North Africa had finished at the bottom of the sea and I was thankful I wasn't with them. Then we heard the most wonderful news: the second front had started in Normandy – D-Day had arrived.

We were stationed close to an airport where aircraft flew to Yugoslavia with guns and ammunition for Marshal Tito's forces, and every evening we watched them fly low over our camp. One evening, we saw one of the planes burst into a ball of fire and crash into the ground. Furious attempts were made to rescue the crew as the ammunition inside the plane exploded and sent bullets flying everywhere, but only the pilot was saved.

I still continued with my duties as a battery clerk and one day, shortly after we'd had a unit photograph taken, we were ordered to move again. This time we found ourselves in 'Castle by the Sea' in the region of Tuscany. Shortly after our arrival, we were told we were to receive a visit from a VIP – Field Marshal Alexander who had commanded many different armies during the war.

Among other things, Alexander, under the American General Eisenhower, had commanded the allied invasion of Sicily in July 1943, when he controlled both General Montgomery's 8th Army and American General Patton's 7th Army. Now, he was to address us in what turned out to be a large sports arena.

Alexander was well known and well liked by the troops, and adopted a casual approach when addressing the men, his hat usually sitting at a jaunty angle on his head. That afternoon he told us to break ranks and gather round as he laid down some of what was going to happen in the future and told us how the war was proceeding.

Not long after the Field Marshal's visit, my name appeared on orders for a move to another unit and I was sent to another transit camp near Naples at a place called Bianco. I said farewell to many of the men I'd known for almost four years and complete with my kitbag and rifle, boarded the lorry for the station. The train stopped and started throughout the journey as the Germans, during their retreat, had adopted a policy of destruction that included blowing up railway lines, but eventually I reached Bianco and made my way to my new home.

It was a large camp and I sensed a sad atmosphere. One of the first sights I saw was six blind soldiers, being led by a corporal to the canteen and I wondered how they would fare in the coming years when all this was over. I booked into the guard room and reported to a sergeant who eventually found me a tent and I settled in for a few days before visiting Naples.

Things were much the same as they'd been when I'd first arrived in the city after we sailed from Egypt. There was destruction and poverty everywhere and many children still slept in doorways, dressed in rags when they weren't begging for food on the streets. But inside the Royal Palace, some of us could escape the horrors for a short while.

At that time, the palace was used as a recuperation centre for wounded soldiers but it also acted as a NAAFI, and there was a cinema, a restaurant and a laundry where you could have your clothes cleaned and pressed. The palace opened at 10:00 and when you went through the doors, you were faced with two elegant marble staircases that took you to the floors above where the balconies overlooked the Bay of Naples. It was possible to spend the whole day inside the palace and on some of my free days I did just that, to escape the drudgery of camp life. But there was always a surprise just lurking round the corner.

I was one of a party chosen to represent the British Forces at a parade in Naples. Our uniforms were scrubbed clean and our khaki drill shorts were starched to the point where they could stand on their own. On the day in question, we were not allowed to wear them on the journey into Naples and were ordered to change out of our old clothes and into the newly cleaned, pressed and starched uniforms on the back of the trucks as we drew closer to the 'parade ground.' The trucks were open and our changing from one uniform into another as we travelled through the streets brought howls of laughter from the local population who must have thought we were all crazy.

We took up our position to be inspected by the Brigadier, and as he came along we drilled as commanded until we were told to 'present arms'. The last action you perform when doing this drill involves slapping the rifle's sling and ours had so many layers of blanco rubbed into them that cloud of fine white dust rose into the air and then settled on our shoulders like dandruff. But for that incident and the changing in the back of the trucks, the day went well.

Not long after the blanco fiasco, I was told I was to be instructed in all aspects of mines and booby traps and for seven days I learned how to defuse various types of bombs and was 'killed' several times in the course of my instruction.

CHAPTER NINE

Suddenly, I was pulled back from my reminiscences to the present day by a loud swishing sound coming from the door to my right and slightly back from the seat where I was sitting. To my horror, a uniformed arm appeared on the back of the seat in front of me and I caught a glimpse of an official-looking hat, as the bearer of the arm leaned down over my right shoulder. Close to panic, I took a deep breath and looked out of the window.

'You should know better, Father,' a deep voice said, and when I looked around the owner of the voice, a tall man wearing a very official-looking uniform pushed himself upright and walked slowly away from me towards the front of the coach. I stared after him until I heard another voice speak.

'It's your cigarette,' a voice from the seat across the aisle said. 'You're smoking. He's the train manager. You're not allowed to smoke in this coach. There's a smokers' coach at the rear of the train.'

'Sorry,' I said, looking around for somewhere to put my cigarette out.

'Put it in here,' the voice from across the way said, handing me as plastic cup with the dregs of what passed for coffee in the bottom.

I threw the stub of the cigarette into the cup and heard the hissing sound as the liquid met the heat.

'I'm sorry,' I repeated. 'I didn't realise.'

'Smoking's a form of anti-social behaviour nowadays, Father,' the voice said. 'Maybe you should consider quitting. I did six months ago. Still feel like one every now and then, but so far so good. It was quite difficult in the beginning, but now I appreciate the health benefits.'

'Health benefits?' I asked, bemused by what he was saying.

'Sure, he said. 'Heart disease, cancer, that sort of thing.'

'Cancer?' I echoed.

'That's right, Father. Smoking causes lung cancer and heart trouble and a load of other bronchial diseases.'

This was all news to me. In my time, smoking was seen as fashionable and sophisticated, something celebrities and other famous people did. Churchill, Clark Gable, Humphrey Bogart, Bette Davis; all the big Hollywood stars smoked and so did everyone I knew, including my doctor. In fact, magazines and films of the day carried adverts that said more doctors smoke Camels than any other cigarette.

'I'm sorry,' I said. 'I wasn't aware of that.'

'God, Father,' he said, 'if you'll excuse the expression, but where have you been for the past twenty years, in a monastery?'

His question troubled me and I struggled for an answer before I blurted out, 'Yes, that's right …a monastery. A monastery in Italy.'

It was clear my answer embarrassed him slightly but it let me off the hook.

'I'm sorry, Father. I didn't mean to be rude. I meant it as a joke. So, you really were in a monastery?'

I was sorry I'd lied but I realised I couldn't retract what I'd said, and in any case it was as good an excuse for my ignorance as any. For the next couple of minutes, I gave him my idea of what it was like to live in monastery for over twenty years. It was of course all pure invention, apart from my description of a monastery in Italy I'd visited during the war. This seemed to convince him and allay any suspicions he may have had as to whether I was a real Priest or not.

As the journey progressed, we chatted about this and that but I learned to let him do most of the talking, for fear I would say something that would give me away. He told me all about his job as an IT consultant, which apparently meant he knew a great deal about computers and telephone systems, and travelled around the country a lot. Much of what he said made absolutely no sense to me whatever, but I could tell that this didn't matter and he liked to talk about his work, so I let him carry on without interruption. Although I was happy to listen, I was even happier when the train pulled into Peterborough station and he got off.

Shortly after the train pulled out of the station to resume its journey north, the coach began to fill up rapidly with people looking for somewhere to sit. Just as a man made to sit on the empty seat to my right, two officious-looking men directed him elsewhere. I noticed that the man didn't object, having been shown some sort of identification by one of the men. My heart went into my mouth when the taller of the two leaned over and whispered in my ear.

'Will you come with us, Father?' he said, and stood back indicating I should follow his colleague into the coach next door. My heart sank as I rose from my seat and I was depressed by the thought that I had been discovered before I'd even made it to the Scottish border. The train was still moving and it was clear that I had no option but to do as I was asked. Maybe I could bluff my way out of it, I thought, so I decided to co-operate without any fuss and followed the smaller of the two men, with his companion at my back, through the automatic doors that led into the coach next door. When the doors closed behind us the man in front stopped and the three of us ended up standing in the small vestibule between the two coaches next to the toilet door. The smaller of the two pulled a wallet from his inside pocket, letting it fall open in front of me to reveal his identification details.

'Railway police, Father,' he said. 'There's an old chap in the coach through there who's became ill. It looks like he's had a heart attack. He's quite delirious and has been asking for a priest. The train manager alerted us that he'd seen a Priest in Coach D, which led us to you. Can you see to him? I think he believes he's dying. We've alerted the hospital further down the line and there'll be an ambulance crew at the next station. We should be there in about fifteen minutes. Meanwhile, can you see what you can do?'

'Of course, of course,' I said, with such a feeling of relief that I wasn't being arrested that I forgot all about the fact that I knew as much about administering to the dying as flying in the air. Having no idea what I was letting myself in for, I confidently indicated we should proceed into the next compartment. When we entered through the doors, the coach was empty, save for two railway staff and the old man. He was seated upright, facing me on the outer of two seats with a pillow under his head and his knees and legs covered by a railway blanket, which I presumed was borrowed from one of the train's sleeper compartments. The girl I'd seen earlier pushing the tea trolley looked up as she heard us approach.

'Here's a Priest to see you,' she said, letting the old man's hand go and making way for me to get next to him.

I sat in the seat opposite him and took hold of his hand, holding it tightly. He was clearly very unwell. His face was ashen grey; his breathing shallow and erratic and he seemed to drift in and out of consciousness. I stroked his forehead and leaned close to him in the hope that the others couldn't overhear me, but I noticed they'd withdrawn further up the coach, respecting the old man's privacy. I whispered some of the basic Latin I could remember from my schooldays and said a silent prayer. Father Flaherty hadn't prepared me for this eventuality and after I'd finished I hoped God would forgive me and the old man would survive. It seemed like an age before we arrived at Milton Keynes, but he was still breathing when the ambulance crew boarded. I released his hand from mine and moved out of the way to let the medical team go about their business. Firstly, they gave him a quick check over and then produced a variety of equipment from black cases, some of which I recognised from my time in hospital. Within a few minutes, I was conscious that the old man seemed to be breathing a bit easier and the ambulance crew helped him onto a stretcher and removed him from the train.

'I think he'll be okay,' one of the crew said as they carried him off. The words almost brought me to tears but I gathered myself together.

'I hope so,' I replied.

'Well thanks, Father,' a voice spoke up. It was the taller of the two railway policemen. He held out his hand.

'We're getting off here,' he said, to my relief. 'I hope the rest of your journey is safe and uneventful.'

'Thank you,' I muttered and made my way back to my seat in the coach next door, elated by my escape.

I must have dozed off and was later awakened by the jolt of the train as it made its way out of Crewe station. In my haziness, I noticed that a young girl was occupying the seat across the aisle and I assumed she had just boarded the train. She was speaking on her mobile phone and when my eyes focused properly it was clear that she was somewhat distressed. When she ended her conversation, she threw the phone angrily into a small bag she was holding on her lap, closed the bag and began to sob. My reaction was to turn away and look out the coach window. When I did so, I caught sight of her reflection in the glass. She was still sobbing and dabbing at her eyes with a sodden tissue. I averted my eyes and watched the landscape flash past, but every second or so they were drawn back to the girl. Finally I rose from my seat, crossed the aisle and sat opposite her.

'Can I help?' I asked, but she shook her head from side to side without looking up. 'Maybe it would help if you spoke about it.'

This time she raised her head and looked up at me. She was an attractive girl with jet black hair and large, deep brown eyes.

'I'll be all right, Father,' she said.

'Can't you tell me what's wrong?' I asked. 'Maybe I can help.'

She never replied to my question, but after a few moments she began to regain her composure.

'I've just had some bad news, that's all,' she said. 'I've just been told my grandfather died this morning and I'm on my way home.'

I said the usual things one says under such circumstances and, remembering Father Flaherty's advice, I allowed her to continue. She went on to tell me she was a drama student at a university in Crewe and had just been told that morning that her grandfather had died suddenly. As she related her story, it became clear that the old man had been more like a father to her. Her own dad, she told me, had been killed in a mining accident before she was three years-old. She came from Wigan and for generations the men in her family had worked in the mines and the women in the mills. In fact, she said the last mill in Wigan had closed in the year she was born, the May Mill in 1980. She was the first of her family to go to university and said she'd been encouraged by her grandfather who, although he'd left school at the age of twelve, was a passionate believer in education and had taught himself to read and write in his teens. His favourite subject was history, especially the history of working-class movements, and her eyes lit up when she told me that on cold winter evenings, when she was a little girl, her grandfather would sit with her in front of a large coal fire, and tell her stories about the miners and their struggle against the pit bosses.

From this she learned a great deal about what conditions were really like for miners and their families in those days. The old man also liked to tell her the story of her dad who, when he was about six years-old, had asked him what nationalisation of the coal mines meant. Not wishing to complicate his answer for the child, he simply said it meant that people like him now owned the coal. To his horror, when he came home from the pit the next day, the boy and his friends had filled his back garden with coal they'd stolen from the pit. Apparently, her dad had told his young friends that it was all right to take it, as his father had said that after nationalisation it belonged to the people.

Just before we arrived at Wigan, she took her mobile phone out of her bag, switched it on and made a call to her mother, who I learned was meeting her at the next station. When the train came to a stop she rose from her seat.

'Thank you, Father,' she said.

I nodded silently and watched her as she walked along the

corridor and through the coach door. As we pulled out of the station a few minutes later, I saw her standing on the platform with an older woman, who was clearly her mother. She was watching the train go past and when my carriage drew level she waved and I thought I detected a hint of a smile. I smiled back weakly and settled down in my seat, closed my eyes, and drifted off to sleep.

'Preston, next stop Preston.'

I awoke with a start at the sound of the train manager's voice announcing we were pulling into Preston station. Suddenly, I was driven by the desire for a cigarette and I remembered there was a smoking carriage at the rear of the train, so I made my way along the corridor. I expected it to be full, but when I arrived in the coach its sole occupants were two young men dressed in football colours, smoking and drinking beer from a can. I sat a few seats back from them and lit up a cigarette.

'Are you all right, Father?' one of them asked, in a broad Liverpool accent. 'Do you want a beer?'

I was half-tempted to say yes, but I resisted the urge.

'No, thanks,' I said. 'Are you on your way to a game?'

'We're playing Carlisle in the Cup tonight,' the one with the beer can said.

'Who is "we"?' I asked.

'Christ, Father,' the other one said. 'Where have you been? Liverpool! Who else?'

'Don't know much about football,' I explained. 'I've never been much of a sports fan.'

'In Liverpool, football isn't a sport, Father. It's a religion. Remember what Bill Shankly said: "Some people think football is a matter of life and death. I assure you, it's much more serious than that." That's what Shankly thought.'

'Too right,' his mate chipped in.

Before I could say anything, I was distracted by the noise of a tea trolley being pushed along the aisle. The girl who had helped the old man before had resumed her normal duties. When she drew level with my seat, she stopped.

'Would you like a cup of tea, Father?' she asked.

'Thanks, that would be nice,' I said. 'Incidentally, you did a grand job back there.' I told her. 'I think the old man will probably be okay.'

'All in a day's work,' she said. 'That was my third heart attack in the last ten days ... well, not my own. You know what I mean. We got two to hospital but the other chap didn't make it. He died on the train. It's very frightening when something like that happens. It makes you think. Here one minute and gone the next.'

'Christ, would you listen to you pair,' said one of the football fans. 'Bloody depressing. Does nobody ever get born on the train?'

'That happens as well,' she said. 'I've dealt with births and deaths in this job.'

'Well, that's life,' the fan said. 'The birth-death cycle.'

I don't know why, but the use of the phrase disturbed me. I could think of no reason why it should have, but it did. I also thought it was a peculiar thing for a football fan to come out with, especially one who only a few moments before seemed only to be interested in football and beer. As if he'd read my thoughts, the fan who had used the phrase spoke,

'I wanted to be a priest, when I was a young boy growing up in the Irish quarter of Liverpool,' he said. 'I'd be Father

John Connolly now if I'd stuck at it, but I left. I lost my faith I suppose.'

I don't know where it came from but I found myself saying that I didn't think people ever lost faith really but simply misplaced it for a while.

'It'll probably find you again,' I said.

'Maybe, Father, maybe. Incidentally, do you have a name? I'm John, as I said. My mate's Alistair.'

The question threw me for a moment or two.

'Name?' I repeated. 'Name? Err, yes. Michael! It's Michael. Michael O'Brien.'

I noticed that when John said he wanted to be a priest, his friend Alistair had looked very bemused and finally he spoke:

'Priest! You?' he said, his voice filled with incredulity. 'You never ever told me you wanted to be a priest. I've known you for years and you never ever said. Are you taking the piss?'

It sounded a fair enough question and I waited for John's answer and I wished I hadn't.

'I got as far as my seminary,' he replied.

'What's a seminary?' Alistair asked.

'Tell him what a seminary is, Father,' John said.

I had no idea what it was, but John expected me to know and with my luck it was likely to be something basic that any real priest would be able to explain, without any difficulty whatever. My mind raced. If I couldn't come up with an explanation, I may raise a suspicion in his mind as to whether I was really a priest at all. I searched around my brain until I finally found an answer.

'Perhaps you should explain,' I said to John, 'and I'll see how much you remember of your training.'

Thankfully, Alistair came to my rescue.

'That's right, why should the Father tell me? You tell me. You're the one who said you wanted to be a priest. So what's a seminary? Father will say if you're telling the truth.'

'It's a school, you dummy. A theological school for the training of priests, ministers, rabbis that sort of thing. I was going to study theology, philosophy, the humanities – all of that. Anyway, in the end I became a plumber. People always need plumbers: they don't always need priests. Besides, that was years ago and if you mention it to any of our mates, I'll kill you.'

'Some priest you'd have made,' Alistair said and continued in a broad fake Irish accent, 'So, you'll be for killing people now is that it? To be sure, is that not a terrible way for a priest to behaving?'

Both of them laughed and it was obvious to me that they were the best of friends but I could understand why John had never told his pal of his earlier ambitions. I was glad this seemed to bring an end to any further discussion on the priesthood for the time being.

I remained in the smoking carriage, chatting with the two boys and by the time they waved goodbye in Carlisle station I knew more than most people about the history of Liverpool Football Club. When they left the carriage, I walked through the corridor back to Coach D to find it completely devoid of people. I re-took my old seat and sat watching the landscape rush by. As we crossed the border into Scotland I felt myself nodding off and soon I was asleep.

For the next hour or so, I drifted in and out of a pleasant

sleep, oblivious to everything around me until I was jolted wide-awake by the train shuddering to a halt.

'Motherwell,' I heard the announcer say. 'Next stop, Glasgow Central. Please remember to remove your bags and other personal belongings when alighting from the train.'

This meant I was only about fifteen or twenty minutes from the end of my journey. I rose from my seat, pulled down my bag from the overhead shelving and headed through the automated doors into the toilet. Inside, there was barely enough room for me and the bag but I made do as best I could. I exchanged my black trousers and black leather shoes for a pair of blue denims and white sports shoes. My white collar and black shirt gave way to a pale blue sweatshirt and I hung a brown leather jacket on the handle of the toilet door, whilst I stuffed the clothes I'd taken off into a black plastic bag. With a small pair of scissors I began to clip my beard and finished the job with a razor blade, cold water and some ordinary soap. Slowly I began to reveal the face of Peter Hunter, but I did not experience the same shock and disbelief as when I'd first confronted my new identity in the hospital. In fact, I began to think it wasn't such a bad face for a man in his early fifties. Sure, there were a few wrinkles here and there but apart from that, it was a face much like any other.

I began to think that if I'd been involved in a mine accident or been badly burned during the War, I would probably have had to learn to live with a different face and get used to it. Besides, I could always grow the beard again if I wished. When I was satisfied with the transformation, I opened the toilet door and had a quick look around before entering into the space between the coaches. All was quiet, so I leaned against the wall next to the train door, lowered the window and threw the black bag containing the priest's clothes out into the night, picked up my travel bag and made my way along the corridors to the front of the train. Most of the coaches were empty, save for the odd person preparing to alight in Glasgow, but as I reached the last coach I saw the female attendant who had assisted with the old man at Milton Keynes approach me along the corridor. I sat down in the nearest seat to let her through and was happy with my changed appearance when she didn't give me a second glance.

A few minutes later, I alighted from the train in Glasgow Central Station. There was no one at the ticket barrier, so I walked across the concourse until I stopped for a moment before a large Howitzer shell from the First World War that had been made into a charity box. Searching for a few of the strange-looking gold-coloured coins I'd been given by the priest, I put a couple into the slot and walked out through the large station doors into the street. Apart from my time aboard the Mooltan in Greenock, this was my first visit to Scotland and I retrieved David's rough map of the area from my jacket pocket, across the road from a taxi rank. David had explained that the centre of Glasgow had been built on a grid system and it was relatively easy to find your way around. This proved to be sound advice and I made my way north up Hope Street, turned left into Sauchiehall Street and headed for David's flat. When I left the station I'd been tempted to board a taxi until I remembered what David had told me about using public transport.

'Taxi drivers have prodigious memories,' he'd said. 'They remember where and when they dropped you off, what you were wearing, who you were meeting, why you were visiting the city, how you got there and a load of other information you didn't know you gave them. They garner all of this information from you without you even noticing it. Walk, that's my advice.'

In any event, it was not an unpleasant evening for a walk and David's directions were clear and easy to follow so within about twenty minutes I was climbing the stairs to the third floor of a building at the corner of Elmbank Street and Sauchiehall Street. When I arrived outside the door of the flat, I fumbled around in my wallet for the key and heaved a sigh of relief when I found it, turned it in the lock, and the door clicked open.

Inside the flat, there was sufficient light coming from the street lamps outside to enable me to discern that it was a small dwelling with a lounge, kitchen, bathroom and a single bedroom. I judged that the door facing me allowed entry to the bedroom and went inside to find I was correct. I threw my bag on the floor, fell down on the large double bed and lay back thinking over my last few days and my eventful train journey, before I finally fell asleep, exhausted by the events of the day.

CHAPTER TEN

I spent the next couple of days getting to know my way around the flat and the local area. The flat was on the top floor of a three-story building at the corner of Sauchiehall Street and Elmbank Street, with windows that overlooked both streets. As you entered the front door, the bathroom lay to the right, the living room to the left and the single bedroom straight-ahead. There was also a door to a large walk-in cupboard in the small hallway, next to the bathroom whose walls were lined with bookshelves. It seemed that there was a book, magazine or journal on every subject you could think of: politics, philosophy, law, theology, religion, science, and mechanics were all represented. There were encyclopedias, dictionaries, reference books, language books and almost anything else you could imagine.

There was no television in the flat but there was a radio and a music system that I had difficulty operating, but I managed to get the radio going and the familiar tone of a BBC presenter brought an unusual feeling of comfort. The lounge had a large black leather sofa, two matching armchairs, a small and plain mahogany coffee table, a fireplace with a three bar electric fire and a telephone sat on to another small table next the fireplace. Leather cushions were scattered about the place but there was little by way of ornaments or pictures on the walls apart from a Taiwanese batik and an Australian boomerang that turned out to be a genuine piece of Aboriginal art. In the far corner, to the right as you entered from the hallway, there was a slim breakfast bar with a couple of high stools. Behind the bar lay a worktop with a hob, and what I learned was a microwave oven. Beneath the worktop, a small fridge and what looked like a machine for washing clothes stood side by side. Some sunken cupboards on the wall above held general foodstuffs like salt, sugar, tea, tins of soup, beans, spaghetti and various other cartons and packets as well as pots, pans and cutlery. It was clearly a man's abode save for the fact that it was immaculately clean and tidy.

I never left the flat on the first day and spent most of the time getting to know where everything was and how things like the hot water, central heating system, kitchen equipment and the like worked. The rest of the time I spent reading or listening to the comforting voice on the radio which was the only thing that appeared much as it had been all those years ago.

On the second day, I ventured out to buy some milk and a newspaper and found myself exploring the local neighbourhood before I returned to the flat. Local residents were certainly not short on facilities: within a few hundred yards of each other there were a number of restaurants and pubs, a casino, a betting shop, a theatre, a dance hall, a couple of churches, and what I learned was one of Europe's largest public reference libraries, locally referred to as 'The Mitchell'. There was adequate access to transport with a number of buses passing through regularly, a taxi rank and a railway station. In any event it was sometime later when I returned to the flat, but there were no messages on the answer-phone and so far no one had called my mobile.

At first, I was a bit concerned that I hadn't heard anything from David or Father Flaherty since I'd left London, but I eventually decided that no news was good news and expected someone would contact me sooner or later. Meanwhile, I had somewhere safe and warm to sleep, food to eat, and plenty of facilities outside the door to keep me occupied. No sooner had I arrived at this conclusion, than I felt the mobile phone vibrate in my shirt pocket. I removed it and pressed the answer button but I didn't say anything until I heard David's voice.

'Are you there, George?' he said. 'It's David, David McIntosh, can you hear me?'

'Hello, David,' I replied, and after some chat about how we both were, how the trip from London went, how I was feeling and so on, he suddenly hit me with the news.

'As far as I'm concerned,' he said, 'the police clearly have no clues whatsoever as to where Peter Hunter may be. In private, I know the top brass think he's escaped overseas but they won't say that publicly. To be honest George, I don't think they have the manpower or other resources to look that hard for you and are probably relying on you making a mistake or some alert member of the public calling them with information.'

This sounded like good news to me until he continued, 'I'm running a piece in tomorrow's paper,' he said. 'It'll say you've been in touch with me and told me the whole story. I've said in the piece that I don't believe you are Peter Hunter, although I don't have any idea how this can be possible, but I believe you to be someone else no matter how fantastic it may seem.'

'And then what?' I asked anxiously.

David, I suppose having detected the anxiety in my voice, laughed before he answered.

'Then we wait for the shit to hit the fan,' he said. 'I expect the police to come storming into my office armed with a variety of warrants and threatening me with all sorts of legal injunctions, or charges of harbouring a criminal, perverting the course of justice, all that stuff.'

'Doesn't that concern you?' I asked quite innocently.

He laughed again. 'Of course not. It would, if they were serious, but it's just a game. Besides, I've heard it all before. We live off each other, therefore we're dependent on each other. The relationship between the police and a journalist is that of the relationship between a dog and a lamppost. Politicians are the same. I expect they'll put me under surveillance, bug my phone, and anything else they can think of, but they'll draw the line at an actual arrest. Anyway, to make sure you don't give the game away, don't call me on the mobile. I'll call you whenever it's necessary. Try to relax, lay low and stay away from people unless contact is absolutely necessary. I've included an email address in the article for people to get in touch with their views on the story, so I expect we'll get some real crazy theories but something may turn up – who knows? The position is mad enough as it stands so we need all the help we can muster. Okay, George, stay calm, I'll be in touch.'

The phone went dead and I mulled over what he'd said. Calm wasn't exactly how I was feeling at that moment. I didn't like the idea of picking up a paper the next day to see my photograph beside lurid descriptions calling me a serial killer, psychopath, and all the other standard jargon tabloid journalists use to sensationalise something that is already sensational. On the other hand, I knew deep down that something had to bring the situation to a close. I couldn't live the rest of my life on the run from the police and society in general. The article itself, of course, would not bring a conclusion but perhaps the beginning of an end. I made some tea, sat by the window and watched some people below enjoying their lunch in the King's Café and others having a drink in the bar across the road. They were doing the normal things that people do, and I longed for their normality.

Around six that evening, I made my way to the Mitchell Library and went on the hunt for a selection of books about the years from 1945 to the present day. Sometime later, as I sat reading and jotting down notes, I was struck by the thought that I now probably knew more about the changes to British society and the world in general over the past fifty or so years than those who'd lived through them. Since my escape from the hospital, I'd spent many days and hours learning about the present and how our country had reached this position, so much so that I felt confident that I could handle this changed environment, if I could only solve the mystery of who I really was. I reached over and pulled a large reference book towards me and as I did so, it fell open and a piece of paper fluttered to the floor. I bent to pick it up and noticed it was a leaflet extending an invitation to all and sundry to attend services at a nearby Spiritualist Church. The leaflet gave some basic detail about spiritualism and mediums and advised that light refreshments would be provided after the service, during which people could get to meet a medium personally and new converts could get to know each other. I put the leaflet on the table without reading any further.

I had no truck with mediums. In my book, they were people who made a living from the dead, by selling glib and easily-led people a cock and bull story about their relatives who had passed on. 'Charlatans and snake oil salesmen' my dad used to call them. People who made a comfortable living out of other people's discomfort and grief. I'd seen mind readers in the old music halls when I was a boy and of course, it was all a trick. They used stooges in the audience and gathered information about unsuspecting victims from ticket sellers, doormen and anyone else they had in their pay. It's amazing what people will tell strangers when they're standing in a queue, and later on, in the excitement of the show, forget they've done so. You can imagine the conversations with the doorman who is walking about keeping the queue in order.

'Just out for a night on the town are we? It won't be long now, the queue's moving quite fast. You don't sound as if you come from London?'

'We don't actually, just visiting. We're from Wales, giving ourselves and the children a little treat. They lost their grandmother last week and it'll help take their mind off things.'

'Sorry to hear that. Had she been ill for a while?'

'No, it was all very sudden. Cancer. Took her almost overnight, she was in her late seventies, so I suppose that's not too bad a life. Poppy, the children called her Poppy.'

And so it would go on. Before long, the doorman had enough information to enable any self-respecting stage actor to put up a convincing performance.

I pushed the leaflet aside without another thought and stretched out in my chair, looking around the library and watching people as they milled around searching the shelves, reading or staring blankly at computer screens. The most popular part of the room seemed to be the family history section, where small groups and individuals were researching archived material and old public records. I suppose, like myself, they were trying to find out who they really were. As my eyes returned to the books and papers in front of me on the table, they were again strangely drawn to the leaflet. One particular sentence caught my eye: 'Monday 7.30 p.m. Clairvoyance' and despite my cynicism I began to consider checking it out.

I recalled that I'd passed the church on my way home from the Kelvingrove Park a few days earlier. Almost without thinking, I rose from the table, put on my jacket and headed downstairs to the library exit. I left the library by the North Street door, turned left into Berkeley Street and a few moments later walked slowly past a row of basement terrace properties until I found myself climbing a flight of stairs that led up into the small church.

CHAPTER ELEVEN

The inside of the small church was much like many other churches I'd visited over the years; with an aisle, rigid wooden pews, circular stone columns, a large stained-glass window, arched roof and a raised dais. What did surprise me was the number of people in the congregation. The hall was almost full but I managed to find a seat in the back row next to the aisle, where I sat down and considered the scene before me.

I wasn't surprised to note that the assembly was predominantly made up of middle-aged and older people, but there were some younger members as well. What was quite surprising, however, was how animated many of them were. My experience of churches was that the congregation sat quietly or whispered to each other before the service began, but here people were quite happy to call out a cheery good evening to anyone they knew, stand about in the aisle speaking in a normal tone of voice and wave across to one another when they spotted a friend. They were like a group of people waiting for a theatre performance to begin, rather than a religious service, but in many ways it was quite comforting. But when the service began, it followed a traditional pattern. There was a welcome, followed by introductions and an opening hymn, followed by a prayer and a second hymn. In my experience, hymns were simply tools used by the minister or priest to move the congregation's thoughts from the mundane to the spiritual and so creating a single energy among the audience. A oneness, if you like. In this respect the spiritualist service was no different from any other church service, but what came next was almost certainly different. Following the second hymn the congregation was introduced to Reverend Jean Robinson, spiritualist minister and medium.

She began by addressing the congregation, on a quite philosophical level I thought, explaining that most of the world's religions believed in life after death. The birth-death-rebirth cycle as she put it, which made me think back to the boy on the train. 'The birth-death cycle,' he'd said, and I remembered being disturbed by the phrase for no apparent reason, and now I experienced the same feeling here in the church. Within a few moments, the feeling had passed and I was able to concentrate on what the medium was saying. To my mind, it was all quite theatrical. She used certain gestures, suggestive language and generalisations designed to generate a response from her audience. As I saw it, most people have lost a relative or friend to cancer, heart disease, lung disorders and a whole host of other illnesses. Most families can trace at least one relative who has been killed in a military conflict and many have suffered the mournful loss of a child. To me, her performance, apart from the religious connotations, was no different from the mind-reading acts I'd seen in music halls and it was clear this was an act, no more, no less.

One after another she called on members of the audience and apparently delivered messages from their dead relatives. Phyllis, who was tragically killed in a car accident, contacted her niece and told her she was happy on the other side. Edward, who passed on only a few days previous, wanted his young son to accept that he was also happy in his new surroundings and so it went on. At one stage the medium's hand, allegedly controlled by a spirit, wrote short messages for selected members of the audience from beyond the grave. It was all smoke and mirrors in my view. I decided I'd had enough and made up my mind to leave, thankful that I wouldn't disturb anyone as I was seated next to the aisle at the very back of the church. Just as I rose, she said something that made me shiver and I was compelled to sit back down.

'I have a message for someone called George,' she said. 'Is there a George with us tonight?'

I let my eyes fall to the floor and sat silent, afraid I would give something away.

'Two,' I heard the medium say. 'Two people have put their hands up but I feel this contact is not for either of them. Is there another George with us? Don't be afraid to put your hand up. No one is in any danger here. I have a message from someone for a person named George. Is there a George with us who is familiar with someone called Peter? Peter Hunter.'

I never heard the rest of what she said as I was gripped by a feeling of terror at the mention of his name. For the next few moments I sat rigid, afraid to move. I clasped my hands so tightly as if in an act of prayer, that I saw my knuckles turn white. I felt the sweat emanate from the pores on my chest and had to make a conscious effort to control my breathing, which was becoming erratic and I feared I was going to pass out. It was the music that restored me and calmed me down and I began to regain personal control. An organ had started playing and I noticed that the congregation was rising to its feet. I clasped the back of the pew in front of me and forced myself to stand, feeling as if my legs were about to go from under me. When the hymn ended, I realised that the service was over. I sat back down and was intent on letting the congregation leave before I did, to give myself time to recover from the shock, but they seemed in no hurry. In fact many of them were heading through a door at the front of the church, to the left of the pulpit, rather than the exit behind me. Others stood chatting in the aisle or remained in their seats, having a conversation with those around them.

'I haven't seen you here before,' a voice said.

It was a few moments before I realised that the statement was addressed to me and when I looked up I was facing Reverend Jean Robinson.

'I beg your pardon,' I said. 'Were you talking to me? I was somewhere else.'

'Contemplation,' she said softly. 'Contemplation! It's good for the soul. I haven't seen you here before.'

'I haven't been before,' I said, as if I was guilty of some terrible oversight. 'I was in the library at the top of the road and I came across a leaflet ...'

Before I could finish she interrupted.

'Compelled,' she said. 'You were compelled to come, I can sense it. Would you care to join us in the church hall? We're having some light refreshments. Nothing too elaborate: tea, coffee, juice, a sandwich or a half-covered chocolate digestive. You're very welcome.'

In my conscious mind this was the last thing I wanted to do, but I found myself answering in the affirmative. She turned round and without another word being spoken I followed her and a group of others through an antechamber at the side of the church pulpit, into a large spacious room teeming with people. A few tables were laid out with white tablecloths holding urns of tea and coffee, bottles of fruit juice, paper plates filled with biscuits and sandwiches, cups and saucers and tea mugs. The scene reminded me of the youth clubs of my day and could have been set in the thirties rather than the 21st century, apart perhaps from the plastic bottles and electric urns. I helped myself to a mug of tea and a digestive biscuit and feeling a bit out of place wandered around the hall musing over what had happened a few minutes earlier. It wasn't long before some of those present introduced themselves and engaged me in conversation and slowly I began to feel a bit more relaxed and I made a small contribution to the general chit-chat saying little, but nodding politely and making appropriate noises. Much of what they said related to their personal experiences of death and contacts they alleged they'd made with their dead relatives and friends over the years, either through a medium or individually. On one hand, you could have been forgiven for thinking them crazy, but on the other they appeared perfectly normal people from many different walks of life. As time went by I met a couple of retired schoolteachers, a lawyer, a doctor, a plumber, a woman who ran her own flower business, another who ran a herbal medicine shop and a couple of young girls who worked in a contact centre, who'd come along with some student friends. It was a gathering that one would expect to meet at any public function from a football match to a theatre concert and none of them looked particularly mad, but their main topic of conversation was by its very nature quite disconcerting as the majority of them swore they'd spoken with dead people.

The medium moved around the room quite confidently, stopping to chat with each group for a few minutes, laughing and saying goodnight to those who were leaving and nodding politely when approached. In every way she was playing the part of a perfect hostess entertaining her friends, but to me it was all part of the act. Inevitably she reached our group and exchanged pleasantries with each of the members in turn, until at one point she and I found ourselves out of earshot of the others.

'You're George Giles, aren't you?' she said quite matter-of-factly. The statement caught me wholly off guard and I tried to feign confusion.

'David,' I replied. 'My name's David. McIntosh, David McIntosh.'

'Very well. David it is, for the time being,' she said. 'But I have a feeling this person was trying to get a message to someone in the congregation and that person was you, although George was the name he used. It was as powerful a contact as I've ever experienced and I'm convinced that George Giles is with us tonight. For whatever reason – perhaps scepticism, fear, apprehension or simple embarrassment, he does not wish to reveal himself. A very understandable approach from anyone who doesn't understand what spiritualism is about and has come to us for the first time. Do you believe in God?'

Her question was so unanticipated I was thrown off guard for a moment. When I regained my composure, I rummaged around in my brain for an answer.

'I was brought up to believe in God,' I said, quite unintentionally abrupt and as if the suggestion that I was conceivably a non-believer offended me.

'Do you also believe in an afterlife? In a life after this one?'

Less defensively I replied that I was raised with a belief in God and consequently a belief in life after death went with the territory. I hadn't, I told her, any occasion to change my mind although like many other people I had my doubts and there were times when I questioned it.

'So we are as one in our belief that there is a life after death?' Before I could respond to her clearly leading question, she continued. 'Which raises the question as to why you are so sceptical of what I do? There is no need to deny you are. It's obvious! I can sense it and I agree it is a perfectly reasonable position to adopt but I fear it stems from ignorance and fear.'

'You claim that you contact the dead. Is that what you mean?' I asked. 'Of course I'm sceptical, but I wouldn't say I was afraid. I've seen many stage performers. I was never afraid of them either. All smoke and mirrors stuff. This contacting the dead business.'

She eyed me closely before she spoke again.

'That, I'm afraid, is a misunderstanding of what a medium does.' she said. 'We do not contact the dead – it is the dead who contact us. Perhaps, if you allow me to explain, it may make the concept of spiritualism a bit clearer. It is a very misunderstood philosophy.'

This was different from anything I'd heard before and I had to admit to myself that I really didn't know that much about people who followed this particular religion, so I nodded my consent and we moved towards a couple of seats at the end of a long table. I poured myself another cup of tea and waited for this new enlightenment.

'Spiritualism proposes that man's spirit survives physical death,' she began, as she sat down waving aside my offer of a refreshment. 'It has always been in man's nature to question what happens after death and Spiritualism proposes it has a definite answer. We believe that the spirit survives physical death and enters a Spirit world which surrounds and interpenetrates our material life. We argue that the truth of this can be revealed under the right circumstances. Spiritualism, as I see it, is as much about the ability to communicate as anything else and I believe that certain people have the ability to communicate with the spirit world and the earth world. But, and this is important to understand, mediums do not call up the dead. It is the spirit world that contacts the earth world, not the other way around. If conditions are right and a spirit is present and willing to communicate and we are willing to receive, then communication can and does take place. This contact may be by way of noises, voices, materialised figures, or the medium may hear or sense the spirit and their thoughts. Spiritualism is a philosophy that simply encourages us to discuss and think about our approach to life. We recognise there is a creative force in the universe and that force is God, so we acknowledge God as our Father. We are in essence each other's brothers and sisters. We come from the same universal life force, which means we are a brotherhood. We support and comfort each other, materially and spiritually. We believe, as do all other religions, that there is life after death. We believe the creative life source can never be destroyed. It merely changes its form or energy, if you like. We also believe in personal responsibility and that after death there is compensation for good that's been done and retribution for evil. Remember the Bible: "he that troubleth his own house shall inherit the wind". As you sow, so shall you reap! There you have it, David. Spiritualism in its condensed form.'

A condensed form she may have thought her explanation was, but it was a lot for me to take in, particularly as my mind was still trying to come to terms with her earlier reference to Peter Hunter and I didn't want to ask her directly about the alleged message. Although I believed she knew I was George, I was not about to confirm it and I sought a way round asking the question directly.

'You say it is the dead who contact you,' I said. 'What do you mean by contact? Do you hear voices in your head, do you see dead people or do you sense them? It all seems very hit-and-miss to me.'

'In what way?' she asked.

'Like earlier this evening,' I said. 'When you said someone called Peter had a message for someone called George. It was all very garbled and confused, I thought.'

I sensed she was a bit hesitant in answering but eventually she replied.

'Sometimes I do indeed hear voices in my head, as you suggest. On other occasions it is more sentient. Much of it is a matter of the interpretation of feelings, language and other things. Is the person who has made contact happy, sad, troubled, disturbed, things like that. For example, the message from someone called Peter Hunter I sensed was from a troubled soul, but not troubled in the normal sense. I felt great anger and I will admit for the first time in a long time I also felt quite afraid.'

'Afraid?' I asked. 'Isn't being frightened something that spiritualist say we shouldn't be?'

'Exactly,' she said. 'We should not be afraid. Not in the slightest. Those who contact us are those who we knew and cared for when they were alive on earth. It makes no sense to be frightened of them simply because they have passed over. They are our friends, our relatives, people we loved. What is there to fear?'

'But you were afraid this evening. You said so yourself.'

'That was very different! Very different! I haven't ever experienced such a deep feeling of trepidation before and I've been a spiritualist for a very long time. At the age of six I began to see a spirit of someone whom I later identified as my grandmother. At the age of sixteen, her spirit started showing me visions of things to come and when I was nineteen I entered into a period of study of the religion. For over twenty years I have been a practising medium and not until tonight did I ever feel such fear when talking with the dead. In fact, I felt I was in the presence of a great evil but it lasted only a few moments and I know that God will protect me from whatever wickedness Peter Hunter represents.'

I was very impressed by her candour and felt for the first time that this was a person I could trust.

'What did he want?' I asked.

She thought for a moment before answering. 'It was difficult to deduce. He seemed to be saying that he wanted back or he would be back. Something about reclaiming his earthly body. He said George would understand. I got the feeling that whoever Peter Hunter was, he is now a very disturbed and angry man. I think him to be an extremely evil person, but I have no real evidence to support that. Did you know him?'

Her answer and her question again raised feelings of fear in my stomach and I felt I could not go on with this conversation and a pressing desire to get away.

'No,' I said. 'I have never met anyone by that name.'

'But you are George Giles, aren't you. You are ...' before she could continue I hastily made my excuses, promised to return to a later session and made my way hurriedly through the church to the exit.

I was halfway down the stairs when it began to rain and I struggled to light a much-desired cigarette. When I eventually succeeded, I drew heavily on the wet tobacco and began walking along the quiet street in the direction of the flat, with my mind in turmoil. Sleep would be difficult to come by this night I reflected, as I rushed through the driving rain. With this thought in mind I turned the corner from Bath Street into Elmbank Street across the road from the King's Theatre. Just as I turned, a car drew up about twenty yards in front of me and a tall man got out, crossed the road and entered the passageway leading up to David's flat. He could, of course, have been visiting any of the other residents in the block but for some reason I held back and took shelter in a doorway adjacent to an Indian restaurant, where I had a good view of the building. I lit another cigarette and looked across and up at the windows of the tenement block to see that the only flat that wasn't showing a light was David's on the third floor. I thought for a moment that I saw a light flash briefly inside the flat, as if someone was using a torch. It could have been the lights from the cars travelling along Sauchiehall Street, reflecting on the window, but it didn't seem likely as it only flashed once and the street was busy with traffic. I stayed in the doorway until I'd finished the cigarette and dropped it at my feet. As I did so, I became aware that the man was crossing the road back towards his car. I left the doorway and headed down the street in the opposite direction of the flat. I crossed over Bath Street and stood in the doorway of a side entrance to the theatre on the corner. I lit another cigarette and looked up the street and the car was still parked with its lights off, but I could make out the outline of the man sitting in the driver's seat from the headlights of passing cars. It was clear that he was watching David's building, so I crossed the road and entered the public house on the opposite corner.

Taking my turn in a queue behind the theatre crowd, I ordered a small glass of whisky and a half-pint of beer and sat near a radiator hoping to dry off my wet clothes. When I left the pub about forty minutes later, the car was still in the same position and the driver was still seated behind the wheel. I turned and went back inside, ordered another drink and asked the barman for the use of a local telephone directory. I found the number I was looking for and made a call from the public phone situated at the far end of the bar, ensuring that I wasn't overheard. The phone was very different from the large black boxes with silver plungers marked A and B found in the old London phone boxes. You had to put your penny in and dial the number, then if someone answered you pressed button A and if they didn't you pressed button B to get your money back. When I ended the call, I drank the second Scotch and went outside positioning myself back in the doorway of the theatre.

I had been standing there for about fifteen minutes, when I saw a police car turn into Elmbank Street from Bath Street and draw up behind the parked car. Two officers got out of the vehicle and approached the offside front door of the parked car. Almost immediately, the occupant of the parked car opened the door and got out. He had a conversation with the police officers but he didn't appear to be asked to identify himself and never produced anything from his pockets. After a few moments he got back into the car, the lights came on, a puff of smoke came from the exhaust, the right indicator flashed and the car moved off, caught the lights just before they turned red, and turned right into Sauchiehall Street. A moment or so later the police drove off in the same direction. It had taken about twenty minutes since I'd phoned them and anonymously reported a suspicious character loitering in a car outside the building.

I left the doorway, crossed the street, entered the close and walked upstairs to the flat. There was no sign of a forced entry and inside everything was as I'd left it. If the man had been inside, he must have let himself in with a key. I began to convince myself that I was probably imagining things and he was most likely waiting for someone else but on the other hand I wondered why, if that was the case, he drove away when the police arrived? Puzzled, I decided to leave the lights off and lie down on the leather sofa. Every now and again I looked out of the window but the street below was empty save for the odd drunken reveller or passing car. It had been a hectic evening and as I tiredly sank onto the sofa, I was again draw back to what now seemed like a former life as a soldier in the British Army.

CHAPTER TWELVE

'All roads lead to Rome,' as the saying goes, and, on my first free day in 1944 after I was promoted to sergeant I was determined to see the city. The first church I saw on the outskirts of Rome was San Paolo. It was a magnificent sight. Later, I headed for the Colosseum and standing at the top of the stairs looking down into the arena, I swear I could hear the sound of chariots and the cheers and laughter as those poor, unfortunate Christians suffered death for the perverted pleasures of others.

At this point of the war Rome was classed as an 'open city', which meant that we could not carry arms and it was supposed to be free from air attacks. However, on one occasion, I was approached by a group of angry Italians who claimed that the British had just bombed a hospital. I told them this was absolute nonsense, but things were quite heated for a while. I wished I'd been allowed to carry my weapon, but the crowd finally dispersed. Whether a hospital had been bombed or not I never found out, but I'm sure it was a piece of German propaganda.

One Friday evening, a British paratrooper was murdered and so the next morning a group of his mates carrying sub-machine guns under their camouflage tunics went into the city intent on revenge. The stillness of the city was broken by the sound of machine-gun fire strafing monuments until the soldiers made their way off when the Red Caps appeared.

In a main thoroughfare, there was an enormous building that served as a NAAFI. It was about four floors high and from above you could look down on the open centre, where an orchestra played and a female vocalist sung the popular songs of the day. Just before you entered, a notice board advised on events that were taking place in and around the city. One that caught my eye was a musical evening at a chateau and the tickets being reasonably priced, I went along with a mate called Max Bacon. As it turned out, it was an outside concert in the magnificent grounds, which regrettably were surrounded by barbed wire. Around two hundred people attended, many of them American troops, but Max and I were the only two British soldiers on view.

The first person to sing was the world-famous opera star Gigli, who gallantly kissed the hand of the lady who owned the chateau at the start of his performance. He was followed by his daughter, Rina, and then came Tito Gobbi. For just over an hour these beautiful voices rang out over a perfect summer's evening and thoughts of war were gone.

Some days later, a few of the soldiers decided on a trip to the Vatican. I was looking forward to the experience and as I entered St Peter's Basilica, I was stunned by its enormity. I was convinced it could have held Westminster Abbey, St Paul's and St Sophia's in Istanbul in this one room of St Peter's. The Pope held his audience in the Sistine Chapel, a most beautiful chamber with the ceiling painted by the great artist Michelangelo. As we entered, we were flanked by Swiss Guards and handed a slip of paper bearing a photo of the Pope. After a few minutes the Chamber became very crowded and when sufficient numbers had entered, the doors were closed.

When we were settled inside, the Pope was carried into the room on a bier by four Swiss Guards and gave his blessings as he moved above the silent crowd. Then, moving to a raised platform, he alighted from the bier and sat on a chair. He was a slight man and spoke very quietly, telling the assembled onlookers how pleased he was to see so many English soldiers, firstly in English, then in French and finally in Italian. After he spoke he raised his hand and blessed us, which I noticed also acted as a signal for the Swiss Guard to assist him back onto the bier and through a door into another chamber. From that day, I resolved to visit St Peter's as often as I could and also the nearby Circus of Nero, where St Peter and other martyrs were crucified. In the centre of the forecourt a large granite pillar marked the spot where St Peter met his end.

I also spent time in the Vatican Museum and the treasures it contained drew my breath away: bibles encrusted with diamonds, sapphires and pearls and cloaks spun of gold, but outside hungry children stood in their bare feet. I once said to an Italian that I thought some these treasures should be sold to feed the people but he shook his head and said: 'we cannot sell our history!'

Another church I visited was the St John Lateran, in the San Giovanni district of Rome. On one occasion, four of us met a priest who directed us to a glass case just below the altar. Inside the case lay a silver cross, which, he explained, was presented to the church by a Spanish princess. Glass had been inserted in the cross, through which you could see pieces of wood, that were said to have come from the actual wooden cross upon which Jesus was crucified. We were also shown thorns said to be from the Crown of Thorns placed upon his head, and pebbles from the stone placed in front of the Holy Sepulchre. I'm afraid when I left I felt like a doubting Thomas, but there was no doubt about the beauty of the church itself. Of course, Rome had not always been a Christian city and in its pagan days the early Christians did not have their own cemeteries. If, which was unusual, they owned land, they buried their dead on it, but otherwise they used underground caves that led to the Christian catacombs that we later visited. The passageways inside were only a couple of feet wide and the bodies were interred in recesses in the walls. It was a very claustrophobic experience and as we passed through we came to a number of small chapels here and there. One in particular I remember had a figure or a painting of Christ, my memory does not serve me well as to exactly which, but we were told that it was possible that the artist could actually have seen Christ, which was quite a thought.

Back in the camp, life continued without incident and I went about my daily business as usual. Most of the staff were very tough characters and in civilian life many of them had been prison officers. One evening in particular, I remember the RSM, who had been on the staff in Dartmoor and rarely indulged in small talk, said that there was no reason to speak to anyone other than to say 'good morning' when you arrived at the office and 'goodnight' when you left in the evening. Thankfully the rest of the staff were more sociable and associated with each other outside of work.

Several months had passed since we'd arrived in Rome and as the festive season approached, we decided to throw a Christmas party for the local children. The officer who had been nominated as Entertainment Co-ordinator arranged for the Army Cinematograph Unit to supply the films; and the men set about making toys with great enthusiasm. It was amazing to see what they made from very sparse materials and the variety of skills was quite humbling. Wooden scooters, cricket bats, doll houses, train sets and a host of other toys appeared daily, and to make it a bit extra special every one gave up their chocolate rations. Soon after noon on Boxing Day, the local children arrived at the camp. We had transport arranged to take them from the gates to the main hall – a donkey that we borrowed from a local farm. The children and their companions sat down to a meal prepared for them by the cookhouse staff and after the meal it was time to start the party. Each child was issued with the same amount of 'toy money' with which they could buy sweets that were priced with little tickets. After they bought their sweets, they were shown into the room where a film show was organised and they sat and shouted and cheered through Mickey Mouse and Donald Duck cartoons while many of us were near to tears. After the cartoons finished Father Christmas, also known as sergeant Fisher, arrived with his sack brim-full of home-made toys and a hush came over the hall. What an absolute joy it was for these war-hardened men to see the children's delighted faces as they walked to the front to receive their presents. When the two children in my care for the day were called out, the little boy got a cricket bat and the little girl a doll's house.

A few days after the party, I visited the ancient city of Pompeii, which was destroyed when Vesuvius erupted almost two thousand years before. It was a strange experience seeing the bodies of people and animals preserved exactly as they fell under a cloud of molten ash. A guide showed me around for a small fee and he pointed out that an election was being held when the volcano erupted and I could see the voting propaganda on some of the walls. Among other things I was shown a fossilised bakery, and inside some of the preserved villas young artists sat copying the wall paintings that looked as if they'd only just been painted that morning. On my way back to Rome, I was offered a lift from an Italian driver and like a fool I accepted. My experience of Italian drivers until then was that they liked to drive fast and this one was no exception. He sped along the country roads and it seemed he never missed a pothole, of which there were plenty in this war-ravaged countryside. I bounced around for what seemed like an eternity until he pulled up in Rome at around 02:00 at a military police depot. Inside, I was offered a comfortable chair for the night and before long my aching limbs were at rest. In the morning a bright and breezy sergeant awoke me about

07:00 with a steaming hot cup of tea and an offer of breakfast. Not long afterwards a truck arrived and drove me back to my camp, where I settled back into my daily routine.

CHAPTER THIRTEEN

I awoke around seven the next morning, lying fully clothed on the sofa, feeling miserably cold having fallen asleep in my damp clothes and having forgotten to turn the heating on. My first thought was that I'd fallen asleep as I recounted some of my time in Italy and I was troubled by the fact that I couldn't remember the name of the village outside Rome where I was stationed, or any event after July 1945. Consoling myself with the notion that my memory was probably affected by all that was happening to me and would come back eventually, I slipped off the sofa, crawled across the floor and switched on the electric fire. When the three bars turned red I began to warm up and lit a cigarette to prevent me from going back to sleep again. After I finished it, I rose from the floor, crossed to the window and looked from behind the curtains down into the street below.

I half expected to see the car from the night before parked across the way, but it wasn't there. The street was busy with traffic as people made their way to work and I held my jacket in front of the fire for a little while before putting it on. I returned about ten minutes later from the twenty-four hour shop carrying a bundle of newspapers, some morning rolls, milk and a packet of teabags. I laid the papers on top of the breakfast bar and leafed through their pages in between frying some bacon and eggs and making a pot of tea. I noted that the Scottish editions of the morning papers hadn't gone overboard on the story about Peter Hunter's disappearance. In fact, where it was reported at all, it was on the inside pages and I was pleased to see there were no photographs. Scottish editors clearly didn't rate my disappearance as the main story of the day, but instead chose between an allegation of an improper relationship between a BBC journalist and a senior Scottish politician and a report of a suspected flu epidemic in Aberdeen. When breakfast was ready, I sat on the stool at the bar, leaned over to turn on the radio and flicked through the newspapers as I ate.

Suddenly, I heard the voice of David McIntosh and I turned, half expecting to see him enter the flat until I realised his voice was coming from the radio. I quickly turned up the volume in time to hear the presenter questioning him on what he knew about my disappearance.

'So you say that the man you interviewed, a man calling himself George Giles, is not Peter Hunter, although the police say that Peter Hunter was never out of their sight from the moment he was taken from Broadmoor to the hospital, from which he later escaped? He is the same man who escaped from the hospital, isn't he?'

'Yes,' was David's sole reply.

'The same man the police say is Peter Hunter, a convicted killer. A convicted killer that you are protecting.'

'He was later declared insane.'

'Well makes no difference in the end, does it? He's a psychopathic killer responsible for the deaths of six women, isn't he?'

'You cannot be responsible for anything, if you are insane. That's the law, basically.'

'Well perhaps, if you want to indulge in hair splitting, but let's move on. You say that you've spoken with this person who calls himself George Giles and you're convinced that he isn't Peter Hunter. That's impossible, isn't it? Unless, of course, the man you've been speaking with is not the same man who escaped from the hospital.'

'It's the same man, but that man is not Peter Hunter. His name is George Giles, of that I'm convinced.'

'By all accounts, everyone involved – the police, the doctors, the nurses, even some of his fellow patients at Broadmoor – all say the man who was taken to hospital for treatment, after falling from a wall at Broadmoor in a botched escape attempt and who later escaped from the hospital is Peter Hunter. All of them! On the other hand, you and you alone say they're wrong and you're correct, although you agree that there is only one man involved here. It's an absurd position, isn't it?'

'Put like that I'm inclined to agree, but nevertheless I'm convinced that Peter Hunter and George Giles are two different people and the man I spoke with is not Peter Hunter.'

'What do the police say about this strange story you've published this morning?'

'I haven't been contacted by the police yet. I expect I will at some point later today.'

'I expect you will, too. Are you expecting to be arrested?'

'That's a matter for the police. Let's wait and see!'

'Well that's all we have time for this morning. My thanks to David McIntosh of the *Independent* and my other guests. I expect David will have a busy day explaining his fascinating piece in this morning's paper in which, as you've heard, he claims that the serial killer who escaped from a London hospital a couple of weeks ago is in fact another person, who was born in 1918. That's it for today, and if you want to comment on anything mentioned on the programme, you can visit our website at www…'

I reached over and turned the radio off before he finished. It was clear from his tone that the presenter didn't believe any of what David said and was using ridicule as a tool to persuade the audience to accept his or his producer's view. In all honesty, it was a position I could have understood, were I not the subject of the story. I thought of calling David and saying I wanted to give myself up. Perhaps I could persuade the authorities, within maybe a year or so that I was not a danger to anyone and should be released. Of course, that would mean accepting that I was Peter Hunter and at that very moment I was beginning to have doubts myself as to who I really was.

Often, usually just before I fell asleep at night, I would tell myself that I was going through a waking dream and when I awoke the next day, it would be 1945. I'd be on my way back to London from Italy, the War would be over and I'd be looking to a future out of uniform. There would be no computers, mobile phones, plastic beer mugs, television or any of the rest of the paraphernalia of the 21st century I'd had to come to grips with over the last two weeks. But it never happened, and now I asked myself how long a dream or a nightmare could last. It was indeed the year 2000; I had to accept that and I also had to acknowledge I was about fifty-five years-old. If I were George Giles, I would be eighty-two. In terms of physical fitness, I could be in my early forties. Peter Hunter, among other things, was a fitness fanatic and had spent most of his time in Broadmoor following a strict diet and exercise regime. He had certainly looked after the body that was now occupied by the mind of George Giles. I, on the other hand, smoked and drank, a little too much at times if I'm honest, and enjoyed good wholesome food like bacon, eggs, butter and potatoes, most of which I learned were now given a bad press. I finished my traditional breakfast, poured another cup of tea and sat in the armchair next to the fireplace, lit a cigarette and began to reconsider my position.

Although it was impossible for others to believe, it was really quite simple. I was one man occupying another man's body: that was the uncomplicated truth. Even if I was mad, to me it was the situation. I fumbled around in the wire basket structure that was suspended from the underside of the coffee table and fished out a pen and some writing paper. On one sheet I wrote the words 'Peter Hunter' across the top. On the next line, I wrote positive on the left-hand side and negative on the right-hand side. I did the same with the second sheet under the name of George Giles. In theory, at least I could choose either identity.

As Peter Hunter, my future would be much more certain. I would be incarcerated in Broadmoor, at this stage for an indeterminate period of time – a clear negative. As George Giles, I would be permanently on the run. As Hunter I'd get three square meals a day, have access to newspapers, television, be able to work in the hospital gardens and have doctors and nurses on call – all positives. As George, I probably wouldn't know where my next meal was coming from most of the time. I'd be constantly on the move, afraid to get involved with people, unable to trust anyone. All negatives. But as I'd never killed anyone I wouldn't have that on my conscience, but then Hunter had no conscience so that was a neutral point. Of course, if I was asked whether I felt remorse, unlike Hunter I'd be able to say yes.

The sheets began to fill up as I wrote, and so far living as Hunter seemed to have more positives than being George. If I gave myself up as Hunter, I thought I might be able to persuade the authorities that I was a changed man. That I was no longer insane, no longer dependant on medication, and could now show deep remorse and regret for the killings and perhaps eventually get released. 'How long would that take?' I wondered, 'two years? Maybe longer, who knows?'

I don't remember how long I spent thinking about the future and writing down my ideas, but I began to develop a headache and decided I needed some fresh air. Thirty minutes or so later I found myself sitting on a bench in Kelvingrove Park. I'd come to a decision, or rather postponed any decision for a week. I'd decided to give myself a week to think it over.

The memory of the man in the car the night before came back to trouble me and I decided if I was going to take a week to think through my position, it would be best if I didn't stay at David's flat. So I set off in search of somewhere to stay. I had enough money to rent a room somewhere for a week or so and later found one in a small hotel in a street off Woodlands Road near Charing Cross. The rent would have been a fortune back in 1945, but turned out cheap at today's prices. The accommodation was clean and tidy and although my room was on the small side it was of no real concern as I had little personal effects to bring to it anyway, and I would only be staying there for a short time. The hotel had a few permanent guests: two Italians who worked in the restaurant business, a Pole who ran a market stall and a couple of builders who were working on a long-term building project in the city. Other guests came and went on an ad hoc basis, mostly salesmen staying overnight. I paid a week in advance and told the landlady, a stout Jewish woman in her early fifties, that I worked with computers which seemed to dissuade her and her other guests from asking too many questions about what I did for a living.

For the next few days, I lived much like a tourist on a visit to the city. I went sightseeing on an open-top bus, taking in some of the wonderful architecture of the city's Victorian buildings. I visited museums and art galleries, and went for walks in many of the city's fine parks. It was on one such walk around a park known locally as Glasgow Green that I came across a sort of social history museum called 'The People's Palace and

Winter Gardens'. Many of the exhibits told the story about the lives of the people who worked in the city's shipyards, factories, shops and offices throughout the years, the types of housing they lived in, how many of them struggled to make ends meet, the city's relationship with trade unionism and the Labour Party. It also had features on their social life, cinema and dancing in particular, as well as other aspects of Glasgow life, all topped off by a large greenhouse featuring exotic palms and a spectacular Doulton terracotta fountain. It was a marvellous place to spend a morning, but it was an odd visit in many ways. Many of the things I saw on display purporting to be relics from the past, such as the Anderson air-raid shelter, were instantly recognisable to me as everyday items and I was more familiar with the prices displayed on the goods in the replica dairy shop window than I was with the price of a pot of tea in the museum's modern café.

After leaving the museum, I took a trip along the Clyde on a former Amsterdam ferry and spent a couple of hours in a small museum that told the story of Glasgow's great shipbuilding tradition through the medium of exhibits and film. Again, many of the exhibits I saw and handled were everyday things to me and not the past in the way they were represented on screen. It was difficult to accept within myself that these were indeed items from a long-gone age, and on the trip back to the city centre, I began to realise that at some point I had to mentally accept that I had 'lost' over fifty years of history and had been parachuted into the 21st century.

Whilst the trips to the museums were educational and inspiring, I also indulged in some less intellectually challenging pursuits like having a beer and some food in a pub or spending some time watching horse racing in a betting shop not far from the hotel. This was quite a change from the days I remembered, when bookies hid up a close or down a lane and ran like hell when the police arrived. On many an occasion they were never seen again, I suppose when unusually the punters had a few quid to collect and they couldn't or wouldn't pay them out. A bank of television screens showed horse and greyhound racing from all around the world and the customers sat in small groups drinking tea and coffee whilst they watched their fancies run in a comfortable and relaxed, but somewhat artificially contrived atmosphere.

Life that week, as I saw it, was quite enjoyable and I felt I had some control over my own destiny, but I knew it couldn't last. At some stage I expected to hear from David or Father Flaherty with news that would bring me back to the reality and remind me that I was a hunted man.

My week at the hotel was almost over and I still hadn't heard from David or the priest. On my return to the flat from a morning walk in Kelvingrove Park, I decided to visit the betting shop for a couple of hours. As I entered through the door the shouts from a group of Chinese punters filled the room as they watched their fancy fall at the last fence when well clear of its rivals. Although I didn't understand a word of Chinese, I could guess what they were saying and for the next hour or so my luck continued in the same vein as theirs. I decided I'd had enough and was just about to leave when my mobile phone rang. I removed it from my shirt pocket, opened it and put it to my ear.

'George?' It was David's voice. 'George?' he asked again.

'Hello, David,' I said, 'it's nice to hear from you.'

'Where are you?' he asked.

'I'm in a betting shop in Sauchiehall Street,' I replied quite innocently.

'A betting shop! You're the most wanted man in Britain

and you're sitting in a betting shop?'

'What does the most wanted man in Britain usually do?' I said, laughing. 'I haven't been the most wanted man in Britain before, so I wouldn't know. Where are you?'

'I'm at the flat. The flat in Glasgow where you're supposed to be. How long will it take you to get here? I have to fly back to London in a couple of hours.'

'Just a couple of minutes,' I replied. 'I'm virtually just downstairs.' With that I rang off and headed back to the flat.

David met me at the door with a smile and an outstretched hand. 'How have you been?' he asked.

It was a simple enough question but the answer was more complicated. Firstly, I told him I'd moved out of the flat and was staying at a small hotel on account of the man I'd witnessed watching the entrance to the building a few days ago. His reaction surprised me as he began to laugh.

'That's your paranoia,' he said. 'That's the girl on the first floor's partner. Every time they fall out, she asks him to leave and a day or so later he returns and begs her to take him back. When she refuses to let him in, he sits outside in the car for hours until she relents. They're a strange couple and it's not the first time he's been moved on by the police.'

'Speaking of police,' I said, 'I heard your interview on the radio. Did they get in touch with you following the broadcast?'

He laughed again and told me they were waiting for him downstairs when he'd left the studio and he'd spent most of the rest of the day answering their questions, but they let him go around four that afternoon.

'They're convinced you've escaped abroad, I'm sure of it,' he said. 'I have a friend who's a press officer with the Met and privately he's more or less confirmed they believe you're in Europe. Italy, most likely.'

'Italy? Why Italy?' I asked.

'Peter Hunter was born in a small Italian village. Pietro Hunter is his real name. His father was a British soldier stationed in Italy during the war. After Hunter's father was summoned back to Britain, his Italian girlfriend refused to move to England, so he brought the kid here and reared him on his own with the help of his own mother and the kid became known as Peter. When he was six years-old his father and his grandmother were killed in a car crash and until he was old enough to fend for himself, he was brought up by the state if you like, and farmed out to a number of foster parents: none of whom he stayed with for very long nor formed any emotional attachments with. He has no friends or relatives in Britain and I suppose if he has any living relatives at all, they'll be in Italy, so that's probably why the police think he may have gone there.'

'Italy,' I thought. Here was another strange coincidence. According to McIntosh, Peter Hunter was born in Italy in 1945, in a village only a few miles away from where I was billeted with the British Army. 1945 was the last year I could remember when I awoke in the hospital, to find that somehow or other I had been transported years into the future. Was there some way I'd managed to travel through time that was related to something that happened in 1945? I dismissed the idea as an absurdity. Time travel was for those with highly developed imaginations and science fiction writers as they came to be called in the thirties. I'd read H. G. Wells' *Time Machine* and other such writings, but they were simple escapism. A good read, but the science was pure mumbo jumbo. Besides, in most of these novels, the characters simply travelled through time to a different era but they remained who they were. This was different: I was one man's mind in another's body. I noticed that David sat quietly as I raced through my thoughts.

'There's some sort of Italian connection,' I muttered.

'Italian connection?' David repeated.

'Sorry,' I said, 'I was thinking out loud.'

'No, go on,' he said. 'What do you mean?'

I explained, as I'd done many times before, that the last year I remembered when I woke up in the hospital was 1945. My last memory was of walking down a sandy road in an Italian village, along with three other soldiers. We were heading back to our barracks to prepare to leave Italy for England that afternoon. We were going home after four years of war. Germany had surrendered and although the war was still raging in the Pacific, the war in Europe was over.

'The 17th of July,' I said. 'The 17th of July, that's the last memory I have of 1945, after that I have no memories apart from those that started from the time I awoke chained to a hospital bed. On 17th July 1945, *reveille* was at 06:00. I got up, shaved, ate breakfast in the mess-hall and reported for patrol duty along with two Scotsmen: John Rogers and Ian Stuart and a mad taffy called David Jones. We went on patrol in the village, but as usual it was only a daily routine walk. Later that morning we were sought out, as we were being shipped back to England that afternoon. Our war was over and we were going home. We grabbed each other, jumped up and down and made our way back to the barracks, our arms round each other shoulders and I remember we were singing a World War I song: *Tipperary*. David, who was at the end of the line, pulled us in the direction of a field that was a short-cut to the barracks and that's the last thing I remember. The 17th July 1945, and it seems as if it was only a few weeks ago.'

I looked at David, who had sat listening intently as I spoke. I felt he looked quite confused.

'Are you all right?' I asked. 'You look as if you've seen a ghost.'

'Maybe not seen one,' he said. 'But perhaps I just heard one.'

Sensing that I had something more to say he nodded that I should carry on.

'That's the last thing I remember until I came round and found myself in the 21st century,' I said. 'I don't know what it is, but I have a very strong feeling that there's a connection between myself and Peter Hunter that goes back to Italy and back to 1945.'

'What possible connection could there be between you and Hunter?' he asked. 'You were a twenty-seven year-old soldier, he was a newborn child. When I told you Hunter's birth date you said you can't remember anything after the day he was born, and it's difficult to figure that there is any connection between you.'

At this point, I didn't know why, I decided to tell David about my visit to the spiritualist church and my conversation with the medium. When I got to the bit about the medium saying that a Peter Hunter was trying to get through to someone called George, he looked puzzled again. I went on to talk about the conversation we had after the service and how she'd said that when Hunter was trying to get through, she felt the strong presence of evil. I related in great detail as much of our conversation as I could remember and as I did so, he scribbled down my words in a sort of shorthand on a large, yellow, writing pad. After I'd finished, David looked up at me and began to say something but he never got the chance.

Suddenly, I heard a hissing sound and the room began to fill with smoke. My eyes began to sting and fill up with tears but before I could take any action, a body fell on me from above and two others took me from behind, pitching me forward on to the floor, my head narrowly missing the coffee table.

'Armed police! Down! Down! Down!' A number of voices yelled over and over again before my world became a blank.

The next thing I remember was being bundled downstairs handcuffed, shackled and roughly thrown into the back of an unmarked van that drew away at high speed. My eyes began to recover and I discovered that if I lay sideways across the van I could prevent myself from being thrown around by pushing my feet hard against the side of the vehicle. I was so disorientated that I had no idea how long I'd been inside the van when it eventually skidded to a halt. The back doors were thrown open and at least six men jumped into the back of the vehicle and dragged me out. Some kind of bag was quickly put over my head and I was marched across some tarmac. Gradually, I heard the sound of what I recognised as a helicopter engine and I was thrown inside the noisy machine and secured roughly in a seat. Within a few seconds, we were airborne. I was aware that there were others seated near me in the aircraft, but I could not estimate how many. No one spoke during the entire journey, which I figured was over two hours. I asked for a drink of water and a cigarette, but no one replied. I asked where I was and where I was being taken to, but these and other questions were met with a stony silence. After a while I gave up asking questions and sat quietly, until we landed in what I later found out was the grounds of Broadmoor Hospital.

Still blinded by the bag over my head and shackled hand and foot, I was taken from the helicopter and bundled through at least three doorways before the commotion came to a halt.

'I'm going to remove the blindfold,' a gruff, deep voice said. 'Don't try anything!'

What he felt I could try, I couldn't imagine. I was bound hand and foot, exhausted by the journey and didn't have the energy to fight my way out of a wet paper bag. I nodded in recognition that I understood. When the bag was removed and my eyes got used to the light, I was alone in what I believed was colloquially called a padded cell. There was no seat, no bed, no toilet facility, absolutely nothing. The floor, walls and ceiling were covered with some sort of rubber material and I tried to get myself as comfortable as I could by lying down on the floor. 'So this is Broadmoor,' I thought, before the exhaustion brought on by the day's events eventually overcame me and I fell asleep, wishing I was back in Italy.

CHAPTER FOURTEEN

Broadmoor, as I was later to learn, was now known as a secure hospital rather than an asylum for the criminally insane, as it was when I was a young boy growing up in London. According to the hospital authorities, the emphasis was on treatment rather than punishment, but that wasn't my experience of the night before. When I awoke that morning, my hands and feet were still bound. I rolled around on the floor until I managed to lift myself up into a sitting position and edged myself into a corner, where I was able to sit upright against the cell wall. I ached all over and my wrists and ankles were particularly painful. Soon, the cell door flew open and a group of men rushed into the room carrying riot shields and roaring at the top of their voices. They surrounded me and yelled that I should remain still. The scene was both frightening and comical at the same time, and I got the impression that they were more afraid of me than I was of them. When the shouting had stopped an eerie silence enveloped the cell and I heard my own voice.

'It may come as a surprise to you,' I said, 'but I don't consider I'm in a position to go anywhere. I ache all over, my ankles and wrists are excruciatingly painful. I want to protest in the most vigorous terms about my treatment and what's more, I could do with a cup of tea and a fag.'

'Code Amber, gentlemen,' I heard a familiar voice call out in a quiet but authoritative tone. A gap opened up between the men, through which Dr Wilson appeared. He stood a couple of feet in front of me and smiled calmly.

'Can you assist Mr Hunter to his feet?' he asked one of the men. There was a clear hesitancy to respond among the guards, but eventually two of them laid their shields against the wall and helped me upright and I found myself muttering a reluctant thanks. When I was on my feet, the doctor eyed me with a puzzled look.

'So, Peter,' he said. 'How have you been since your escape? I believe you've given the powers that be a run for their money. Still, you're back among friends now. So! How have you been?'

'I've been treated better,' I said, nodding my head backwards to indicate my arms were bound behind my back.

'It's a temporary measure,' he said, 'until you're assessed. Now tell me, how have you been since we last spoke? What sort of things did you get up to? How did you cope on the outside, so to speak?'

Ignoring his questions, I again made a fuss about the handcuffs.

'Can we make a deal?' I asked. 'Get me a cup of tea, something to sit on and a few cigarettes and I'll answer any questions you pose. You can keep the manacles on my feet. Hell, you can keep the handcuffs on if you let me have my arms out front. Besides, what bloody damage can I do against this small army you've brought with you?'

He thought before answering and it was clear he was at least considering what I'd said. After a few moments he nodded, took a few steps back and addressed the men.

'Code Green!' he said, and this time it was clear this was an order. Again, there was hesitancy among the men, who in my view as a soldier, were poorly trained. In the army, you obeyed instantly. You didn't take time to think about or question an order, you simply obeyed it.

'Code Green,' he barked loudly and this time there was an

instant response and one of the men turned me around and removed the handcuffs. When my hands were free, I slowly rubbed each wrist in turn and leaned against the wall of the cell below a very small rectangular window. A few moments later, one of the men arrived in the cell carrying a couple of small chairs. The doctor sat down on one and invited me to sit on the other. One by one, the men left the cell and I heard the door slam shut, leaving me alone with the doctor.

'Well, Peter,' he said. 'You've certainly created quite a commotion since we last met ...'

'It's George,' I said. 'George! George Giles.'

He ignored my protests and continued with his questions that came thick and fast: how had I managed to cope on the outside world? Had I taken any legal or illegal drugs? Had I been troubled with voices or hallucinations? Had I committed any acts of violence, got angry with anyone or damaged any property? His questions seemed never ending but I answered them as best I could, mostly in monosyllabic terms. I didn't want to implicate Father Flaherty or David McIntosh, although I already knew that David was up to his neck in hot water after the police had found me in his flat, but as far as I knew they had no information that implicated the priest.

Eventually the subject turned to David and again there was a seemingly non-exhaustive list of questions, beginning with how I'd come to contact him. I struggled with an answer to his first question but he pressed the point.

'What made you contact David?' he asked. 'If as you claim you are not Peter Hunter, how did you know to contact him for help? How did you know about their relationship?'

I thought briefly before attempting an answer. As I went through it, I realised it was not very convincing, but there was perhaps enough truth in it to instil some doubt. I explained that when I escaped from the hospital, I'd lived among some homeless people chiefly along the embankment. I told him that in the mornings I'd steal milk and newspapers from doorsteps, food from shops and market stalls and clothes from charity shops. I also said I did some begging in the streets for money and cigarettes and carried my property around in a large bag I'd managed to steal from an Oxfam shop on Oxford Street. I told him I'd used garages and public toilets to wash up and make myself presentable. When he asked how I spent the days, I told him about my visits to the British Museum where I spent hours trying to make sense of the position I had found myself in and it was during one of these visits, when I was researching Peter Hunter, I came across David's involvement and the books he'd written. He listened politely as I spoke but there was no visible sign I could detect that alerted me to whether he believed any part or none of my story.

'So, you contacted him and he offered to help in exchange for an exclusive story. Is that it?'

The question irritated me a bit. Sure, David would get a story out of my predicament, but I never believed that was his only motivation.

'He doesn't believe I'm Peter Hunter,' I said.

'Can he prove you're not?' he replied.

'Can you prove I am?' was the only response I could make.

'We can, but I wouldn't expect we'll ever have to do so. Whatever your game is, the facts remain that you are who you are. You may have invented this Giles character in an attempt to hoodwink everyone into some false doubt, or you may have actually taken on another personality and believe you are indeed someone called George Giles. However, if that is the case, it is more likely due to a development of your schizophrenic condition. In any event, it is most likely that you will have to remain in hospital, probably for the rest of your natural life. As Peter Hunter, you are diagnosed as suffering from a severe form of paranoid schizophrenia. A type that combines the psychotic delusions and behaviour of paranoia with other symptoms of schizophrenia: hearing voices, hallucinations, disturbed thoughts and lack of emotion. Along with your displayed tendency towards extremely violent behaviour and your extraordinarily high level of intelligence, coupled with the ability to manipulate people, you are indeed a very dangerous person. I do not expect you to be released from here for a very long time, if indeed at all. I think you know that as well as I or anyone else does, Peter.'

With these words he rose from his chair. 'I'll make some arrangements for you to be moved to a secure cell for the time being,' he said. 'It'll have the normal facilities. They'll want to put the handcuffs back on whilst they do so, but that's routine in your case, you know that. Then we'll get you some food. I'll be seeing you to carry out some further assessments over the coming weeks, then things will get back to normal, or as normal as they can be here in Broadmoor.'

He made his excuses and signalled to those outside the room that he was leaving and the door was opened enough for me to see the team of guards were still assembled outside. By now, I was convinced that of the two people in this room, one of them was indeed quite mad and it wasn't me. I knew I was George Giles, but I was also the only person who believed this for a fact and the thought made me hopelessly depressed.

CHAPTER FIFTEEN

Over the next couple of months, I had no human contact with the outside world. I'd been moved back into the main body of the hospital along with other patients, but the news I gained about what was happening in the outside world came from the television and radio in my cell and the newspapers that I read in the hospital library. No one visited me, but I was assured that there was no policy in place that precluded me from having visitors or one that discouraged anyone from visiting. I began to remember David's words, when he'd said that if I was returned to Broadmoor the world would forget all about me. It appeared they had.

As the weeks went by, doctors, psychologists, psychiatrists and social workers subjected me to a number of assessments along with other so-called medical professionals. I was given personality disorder tests that asked questions such as whether I suspected other people were setting out to exploit or harm me. Whether I bore grudges. If I preferred solitary activities or if I was indifferent to praise or criticism by others. Did I experience recurrent strange daydreams or fantasies was a popular question, as was whether I had ever been cruel to people or animals? The latter seemed a ludicrous question to put to a person who'd allegedly murdered a number of women, but they asked it anyway. As far as I was concerned, they still appeared to have difficulty figuring out my mental condition with any degree of accuracy and I was sure at least some of them were beginning to wonder whether they themselves were going mad. Over and over again I was driven by the idea that someone should test their sanity rather than mine. I was also subjected to a number of brain scans, apparently to establish whether I suffered from any neurological damage, but there was nothing conclusive, at least nothing I was ever told about. Case conferences, as the staff referred to them, became a large part of my daily routine and during these I met with a whole range of people from within and without the hospital. I answered their questions as honestly and forthright as I could, but I never got the feeling that they were truly listening. It seemed to me that they came to these meetings with preconceived ideas and had their accounts already written up with just a few bare details to add after the meeting. When I wasn't required to take tests or attend a case conference, I spent a lot of time in the ward with other patients.

Contrary to what I'd imagined a place like Broadmoor to be like before I ever arrived there, the sleeping facilities were as good as some hotels I'd stayed in and there was a large recreation room that, although busy, had a quite relaxed atmosphere. There were board games, a couple of televisions, music centres, books, newspapers, magazines, a table tennis table, snooker table and some keep fit facilities. Although most of the patients had, at sometime, been convicted of a serious criminal offence, in most cases extremely violent crimes, there was a quiet gentlemen's club mood about the place and for the most part the inmates were treated as people with a problem rather than prisoners. Treatment, rather than punishment, was the major aim – and of course the protection of the outside world. Patients, who were 'successfully treated', were moved to regional secure units to be nearer their families and friends, but as I had neither, I expected to remain where I was for some time to come. For other patients, the hope was that they could be released back into society at some stage. Of course, there were others for which no such hope existed, and I unfortunately fell into that category. Although the system would go through the motions and consider me for release in keeping with the hospital policy, it was clear the panel that made such decisions would never approve such a move. No one was going to lay their career on the line for someone like me and legally there appeared to be no avenue of appeal through the courts, so my future was indeed bleak but at least it was certain.

Physically I was fit and well and had adapted some parts of Hunter's approach by exercising and watching my diet. Mentally I felt quite strong, although when I dwelled too long on my predicament I could become quite depressed. I'd basically won the argument that I didn't need medication and after a number of tests Dr Wilson eventually conceded that the former medical regime that Hunter had to follow wasn't necessary any more.

Since I'd been brought to Broadmoor I'd proved I could cope without medication, I could handle my temper, I could sleep without sleeping pills and although my situation may have been quite depressing, I handled it well enough. It was less depressing than shooting and being shot at on my way through Italy, which to me was an event that had happened only a few months before. I didn't exhibit any desire to attack anyone or rail against authority. I displayed a reasonably friendly attitude towards my fellow inmates and my captors, as I saw them. My IQ was reasonable but nowhere near that of Peter Hunter. I passed every medical test I was subjected to and whereas some had a clear scientific credibility – blood and urine tests, brain scans and the like – others were no more than some form of psychobabble, claiming to be able to predict a person's propensity to develop a personality disorder through a series of simple questions to be answered yes or no. Overall, I exhibited no psychotic tendencies, showed no sexual disorientation nor irrational fears or phobias. If the tests concluded anything, they said I was a normal, reasonable man. I was the man on the Clapham omnibus. The man who rolled up his shirts sleeves on a sunny Sunday afternoon and mowed his lawn, whilst chatting amiably with his neighbour next door over the garden wall. How then, one could ask, could someone like this be confined in a mental institution?

The answer, which would come from the doctors, psychiatrists and psychologists, would be that George Giles wasn't a real person, but simply the figment of Peter Hunter's highly developed imagination. Giles was a new personality Hunter had developed because he had reached that part of his life where he couldn't cope with what he really was: a psychotic serial killer. It was all very plausible, but although the system would go through the motions and consider me for release, it would never really happen. The public wouldn't tolerate it for a start, the press would see to that, and it was impossible to imagine that any politician would be crazy enough to support a decision that I was 'cured' and no longer presented a clear and ever present danger to the public. Legally there was no ground to challenge my incarceration and according to Dr Wilson, I was Peter Hunter regardless of what the tests revealed.

'Hunter,' Dr Wilson would say, speaking to his colleagues as if I wasn't in the room, 'in his own mind is someone called George Giles, a character he has adopted as a means of blocking out his terrible and violent past. He is in denial of his true self and, for whatever reason, he can no longer live with the murder and mayhem he's caused. Indeed, to cope with his life, to all intents and purposes, he has become another personality. Now, having completed the transition from Hunter to Giles, he has no memories of past events.'

That was his summing up of my case and no other doctor was about to challenge it, so I would remain under lock and key forever.

'You are Peter Hunter,' Dr Wilson had said to me before

one of these meetings. 'I know you are not putting on a conscious act. I know you genuinely believe you are another person, but that person does not exist but in your own mind. I can only interpret your behaviour as another example of your psychotic disorder, and who can say you won't become Hunter again any time you choose. When the human mind comes under great stress, it often finds unusual ways of dealing with it. Ways that psychiatry and other sciences cannot fully understand. There are many documented cases of people who block out painful memories by becoming someone else. I've seen it in cases of abuse. Presently, we know a great deal about multiple personality disorders, phobia, bi-polar disorder, schizophrenia, paranoia and a whole range of mental disorders and human behaviours. Some very common like depression and some very unusual like your own case. However, we don't know all of the answers. In fact, for much of the time we're stumbling around in the dark, but we can't take any chances with dangerously violent people, and you fall into that class.'

It all seemed simple. In short, according to the doctor, I was really Peter Hunter, and for some reason or other I'd become so overwhelmed with guilt that I couldn't cope with my past and simply invented George Giles to hide behind. Dr Wilson's reasoning seemed sound enough, but it left many unanswered questions. I'd heard of people who had adopted more than one personality, but they couldn't describe their other personality in the same way that I could describe the life of George Giles. If I had simply invented him, as Dr Wilson was saying, had I invented all of the memories that went with it? Where did my mother and father come from? Had I made up all of the memories of my childhood, my school, the holidays, my jobs and the army? Was all of this just Hunter's imagination? I was being asked to believe that, in order to escape from my past life as Peter Hunter serial killer, I had conjured up a whole new life: the life of a man called George Giles. I couldn't really buy into that theory. I wasn't convinced! How could I have so accurately described life in London in the twenties, in some instances down to basic details like the number of a bus on a certain route? It made no sense. Perhaps, I thought, the people weren't real. Maybe I did invent this family or maybe this was Hunter's family seen in a different light. It was all very confusing. Surely I couldn't have imagined real events. I could describe places all over Europe from my time in the army. Hunter wasn't born until 1945 and couldn't have experienced any of these things.

Perhaps his father told him about them, after all he'd also been a British soldier in Italy, but having been told about events by someone else wouldn't explain everything. The Giles family in London, how could the doctor explain them away? Was my wife Olive really Hunter's wife? But there was no record he'd ever been married. In essence, there were always more questions than answers, no matter how hard I tried to get to the bottom of it.

Even if I got some answers, how could I ever prove to anyone else that I wasn't Peter Hunter? It was an impossible task. The doctors held all the aces and I decided that my best course of action was to learn to live with the situation. Accept that there was little chance I would ever leave this institution and try to make the best of the rest of my life. Anyway, I told myself, I had most of the things that mattered in life: food, shelter, and access to medical care. I'd made some friends among the hospital patients and staff and, all in all, life inside was not that bad. I had access to books, the hospital gardens, games, music, radio and television. In fact, it was a damn sight more comfortable than my time in the army. Of course I wasn't a free man, but what was freedom anyway? From what I'd determined over the past few months, what I and other men had fought for (and in many cases died for) wasn't worth the bother. The modern-day society I'd been parachuted into seemed more violent than any other that had gone before.

So as the weeks went past, I became more resigned to my fate and came to more or less accept my providence. Peter Hunter was gone and in his place was George Giles: the antithesis of the evil that was Hunter. Of course, the spectre of Hunter still hovered over the authorities and I was regularly subjected to tests and security measures, but the case conferences became fewer and slowly I was given a bit more freedom to move about the grounds without supervision.

With the help of Dr Wilson, I was allowed to apply to study for a degree and I chose the social history of Europe between the years 1789 and 1945 as my main area of interest. I found the reading quite fascinating and was astounded at the social changes that had come over the world during that period. It seemed to me that so many things that happened then could not have happened at any other time in history. There would have been no French Revolution without the American Declaration of Independence, no trade unions without the rise of a working-class, no Industrial Revolution without an agricultural revolution, no British Labour Party without the trade unions.

To me, it seemed events were already ordained and human beings were merely the instruments through that which was predetermined to happen. Although what I, as an individual, was supposed to make happen within the confines of a mental institution, I could not think. But the world seemed to have some sort of structure. That was the point, and indeed if my theory was true then I concluded that each of us must have a part to play, which begged the question: what was mine?

Until now, events had conspired to turn me into a soldier

and I thought back to those earlier days in the hope that somewhere I would find a clue to my present predicament.

CHAPTER SIXTEEN

On Friday the 1st of September, 1939, dawn came up like any other day, but before the sun set we would be at war; Britain's history would change and neither the country nor its people would ever be the same again.

I was working with George Sully at Waterlow's and our work-bench looked out on to St Leonard's Street which led into the City of London. Suddenly, a newsboy appeared carrying a placard in front of him that held the words in large black type: 'Poland Invaded.' The boy walked on down the street calling the phrase at the top of his voice: 'Poland Invaded! Poland Invaded!' and as he walked out of sight a tingling sensation crept down my spine. My head filled with questions about the future and I wondered whether we would really go to war again, especially after the experiences of the Great War in 1914.

Around me, people seemed optimistic and the feeling was that common-sense would prevail. Some said the invasion of Czechoslovakia and now Poland were one thing, but going against a great nation like Britain was another, and Hitler would probably pull his troops back if we threatened to support Poland. But I wasn't so sure, particularly as Russia had entered an alliance with Germany and Hitler and Stalin seemed a formidable partnership. At home, our only means of obtaining up-to-date news was by a battery wireless set. The set belonged to my brother Ted, but he had given it to Mum and Dad about eighteen months before. It was portable to a point and stood two feet high, nine inches in depth and about fifteen inches across. To get it to work required a high tension battery which cost about 12/6d, making it a costly thing to run. It also needed something called a 'grid bias', and an accumulator that needed recharged every three or four days. There were two dials which you had to fiddle about with to tune into a station, but there were few stations and like everyone else we had it permanently tuned into the BBC.

On Sunday, 3rd September, we were made aware that Prime Minister Neville Chamberlain would make a statement at approximately eleven o'clock that night. I stood round the radio with my mum and dad when the sombre tones of the BBC announcer introduced the prime minister. There was a slight pause and the radio went silent before he began to speak in what I thought was a tired, sad, almost apologetic voice:

'I am speaking to you now from the Cabinet Room at 10 Downing Street. This morning, the British ambassador in Berlin handed the German government a final note, stating that unless we heard from them by eleven o'clock that they were prepared at once to withdraw their troops from Poland, a state of war would exist between us. I have to tell you that no such undertaking has been received and that consequently this country is at war with Germany.'

My mother burst into tears and I said something stupid like it will be over by Christmas, in an attempt to console her. My dad shook his head and sat quietly. Before my mother's eyes were dry a siren went off, but it was a false alarm caused by an unidentified aircraft that turned out to be one of our own. Now our ears were glued to the old wireless set, desperate for news and the following day we learned that the British Empire had also declared war, with Canada, New Zealand, Australia and South Africa among others declaring their position.

A few days earlier, a blackout had been introduced, meaning not a glimmer of light was allowed to be seen from any window: traffic lights were hooded, car lights were fitted with blinkers, and train, tram and bus windows were covered. Streetlights were turned off and people got around at night using little torches that they shone on the ground below them. If someone lit a cigarette in the street at night, an air-raid warden's voice would pipe up from nowhere with: 'put that light out!' and we all walked around day and night with little boxes on our backs that housed our gas masks.

Although nothing much was happening in terms of the prosecution of a war, apart from the RAF dropping propaganda leaflets over Germany during the night urging the German people to overthrow their government, a process of evacuating children began. The first of these began in September 1939 and was called Operation Pied Piper. It was very sad to see these children with their labels pinned to their lapels, many of them bewildered and crying.

With September drawing to a close, I realised that my turn to register for the armed forces was drawing near and I should seriously consider which branch I should join. The Air Force appealed to me, as an air gunner in a bomber, which with the benefit of hindsight was almost akin to committing suicide, but before I made any final decision I was approached by my union official at work. He wanted to know if, after I'd enlisted, I would be prepared to go to France with a printing unit which was being set up to produce propaganda leaflets to be distributed in France. I said I was willing and was told that when I reported to enlist and I should tell them I was signed on for the army's printing section – at least that's what I understood from the conversation.

A week after the Royal Oak battleship was sunk by a German submarine whilst she lay at anchor in Scapa Flow in the seas north of Scotland, I was ordered to report to the local labour exchange. It was Trafalgar Day, 1939. The exchange was crowded that morning with men of my age group all ready to sign up and fight for their country. When it was my turn I advised the clerk that my posting had been settled by my union and I was going printing in France. That posting, I was advised, was cancelled and I would have to go through a medical examination in November to determine if I was fit to join the army. To me this was a disaster, as my preference had been for the RAF but whether I liked it or not I was going to be a soldier.

It was a cold, miserable day when I reported for my medical which was to be held in a requisitioned building in Seven Sisters Road, Holloway, in North London. Inside, the building was crowded with young men and teeming with doctors. In truth it wasn't much of a medical and more or less went along the lines that if you were breathing, you were fit for the army. I was given a slip of paper upon which it was stated I was A1. I was then shuffled off to another room where a white-haired man, complete with a monocle, gestured me towards a chair and asked me to sit down.

'And what branch of the Forces do you wish to go into?' he asked.

'I want to join the RAF.'

'Well, you can't,' he said. 'This medical is for the army.'

'Can I join the Army Service Corps then?' I asked.

'Army Service Corps!' he shot back with his monocle falling out of his eye. 'You're A1!' he said. 'Don't you want to tell your grandchildren what you did in the war?

'But I'm not even married yet,' I replied, and for a moment he looked upwards as if pondering on whether he should have me shot or not before he mumbled, 'You will be hearing at some future date where you're going.'

And so I resigned myself to being inducted into the army.

'Peter! Peter!' The voice awoke me and I became aware that I'd fallen asleep in the hospital library dreaming of my boyhood days in London. 'You have visitors,' the nurse said.

'Visitors! Who?' I asked.

'David McIntosh and someone called Paul Thornton. I know David but I don't recognise the other chap. He's very distinguished-looking. Very tall and quite posh I think.'

I yawned myself awake, stretched my arms and arched my back to bring myself back to life.

'I fell asleep,' I said, stating the obvious. 'Where are they?'

'I've shown them into the main hall.' The nurse replied.

CHAPTER SEVENTEEN

When I entered the hall, which provided a recreation area and canteen outwith visiting hours, I saw David McIntosh seated with another man at the far end of the visitors' room, next to the small canteen shop where visitors could buy tea, coffee, soft drinks and a variety of sweets and sandwiches for themselves and those they were visiting. As I approached, both men stood up to greet me. David stretched out his arm and shook me warmly by the hand.

'This is Paul Thornton,' he said, introducing me to his companion. 'Paul's a lawyer and I've been discussing your case with him on and off over the past couple of months and he said he'd like to meet you, so here we are.'

'I'm pleased to meet you,' Paul said, but I noticed he avoided offering his hand by way of a greeting but used it to indicate we should be seated. My first impression was that he was someone used to getting his own way.

He was a tall man, just over six feet I estimated, and I thought in his middle to late fifties, though it was hard to tell. He was slim, with dark hair showing the first signs of grey here and there. His pale blue eyes drew attention to his tanned complexion and everything about him spoke money and education. He wore an expensive and clearly hand-made dark blue three-piece suit, a shirt that matched the colour of his eyes and dark blue silk tie with a small red motif, held in place by a diminutive pale blue diamond tiepin. His shirt had double cuffs secured by diamond cufflinks, the stones matching the tiepin and you could almost see your face in the shine of his laceless, black shoes. A small, very fine gold chain dangled from his waistcoat, indicating that he carried a pocket watch, and he wore a pair of small but sturdy looking gold-rimmed spectacles. It was clear that whatever kind of legal work he was involved in paid extremely well.

'I'm pleased to meet you also,' I said, 'but I'm not sure why I need a lawyer.'

He ignored my remark and before I could say anything else David spoke.

'So how have you been, George?' he asked.

'It's been a while since I heard from you,' I said, 'and why did you bring a lawyer? An expensive-looking one at that.'

Both men laughed at my remark.

'Paul specialises in libel cases. He works for my newspaper on and off. When we can afford him, that is. Mostly we use Paul's services when what we write is challenged by some wealthy celebrity, whose sensibilities are upset, or by a politician who thinks we shouldn't expose his hypocrisy, or the fact that he's cheating on his missus and using public money to fund his extramarital affairs.'

'I can't think what earthly use I'd have for a libel lawyer. Have you seen what they write about me in the papers? Murderer, psychopath, mental case, nutjob; you name it, they write it.'

'Paul isn't here in his capacity as a defamation specialist,' David retorted. 'He also has a special interest in human rights. In fact, he heads up a charity that funds certain cases. Mostly these are political internment, persecution, torture, imprisonment without trial, miscarriages of justice, cases like those.'

'I see,' I said, and turned my head to face Paul Thornton.

'So what can I tell you?' I asked him. 'What can I say about my rights as a human being? Not a lot, quite frankly. I'm imprisoned both mentally and physically. My mind is trapped in the body of someone else and the body is incarcerated here in Broadmoor.'

Before he answered, he pulled his spectacles further down his nose and looked at me over the top of them.

'I don't have any questions at this stage.' he said. 'David has given me most of the details of your case. Let's just say my role at the moment is simply observational. Besides, I believe David has some interesting news for you.'

I turned to face David, who indicated to the nurse that he wanted to hand me a folded sheet of paper. The nurse, who sat at the next table, chiefly to ensure that visitors did not pass any contraband material to a patient – drugs, weapons, a cake with a file in it, that sort of thing – nodded his agreement and David slid the sheet of paper across the table in my direction.

'Have a look,' he said.

I began to unfold the paper, certain that it was either his latest article on my case or some official document. It was indeed an official document, but not at all what I expected. It was a birth certificate in the name of George Giles, dated 11th March 1918. My birth certificate! I read it through quickly, then again much slower, and after three or four readings I suddenly felt I was going to break down and I pushed it back across the table. Out of the corner of my eye I saw a pale blue, silk handkerchief appear.

'Use this,' said Paul. 'You can hang on to it.'

'Thanks,' I mumbled and dabbed at my eyes with the cold silk cloth. 'I'm okay,' I said. 'Just a bit emotional. Please excuse me. I'm all right!'

'Are you sure?' said David, 'because I have something else. If you'd rather wait for a minute or two? Give yourself time to digest what you've just read ...'

'No! No!' I said. 'Let's have it. What else have you got?'

He produced another folded sheet of paper from his inside jacket pocket but he hesitated before passing it over to me.

'Are you sure?' he asked again.

'I'm fine, really. Let's see what you have, it can't be any more surprising,' I said. But it was.

He pushed it across the table. 'It's a marriage certificate,' he said. 'In your name and that of your wife Olive, dated June 1941.'

'Can I look at it later?' I asked.

'Of course,' he said. 'Keep them both, I have other copies.'

'What does this mean?' I asked. 'What do they prove?'

'By themselves, nothing much. Well, nothing at all really.' It was the voice of Paul Thornton. 'At best, they prove the person you claim to be actually existed, but they do not prove you are him. It could be that you have borrowed a dead man's identity, but there is the question as to how you came to know so much about him.'

'That's because I am him,' I said. 'How else could I know so much about the man? All of the intimate details of his life through school, work, the army, relatives, friends, houses ... all of that? Surely only George Giles himself would know all of that?'

He ignored answering my question with a shake of his head.

'In any subsequent legal action,' he said, 'it is likely that you would have to prove you are George Giles. That would be your burden. It would not be the burden of the state to prove you are not. Such questions are irrelevant. Knowing intimate details about someone's life does not prove beyond a reasonable doubt or on the balance of probabilities that you are that person, only that you know the details ...'

I didn't hear the rest of what he said as I was thinking about what he meant by court action.

'Court action,' I said, 'what do you mean? I was under the impression that all possible avenues of appeal were now exhausted in my case and that was the end of the matter. As far as I know, I can only hope that I will be released at some stage of my life, but that would be at the gift of the government and it is extremely unlikely.'

Paul smiled and for a moment I thought I detected a drop in his guard and he appeared almost human, but it didn't last long.

'Let me worry about the legal aspects,' he said. 'I've been a lawyer long enough to have learned that the best thing you can do with the law of precedent is to ignore it. Anyway, it's such a sterile pursuit as a learned colleague once said. In Lord Haw-Haw's trial; you'll remember him I expect?'

Of course I remembered Lord Haw-Haw, or William Joyce as he really was. We used to listen to his propaganda speeches on the radio during the war and thought him nothing but a fool.

'Whatever happened to him?' I asked.

'They hanged him for treason in January, 1946.'

'But he wasn't a British citizen. How can you hang a non-British citizen for treason?'

'He relied on a forged British passport to get into Germany, so he technically put himself under the protection of the British Crown. That, the prosecution said, gave them the right to hang him. As I said, every decision is challengeable, it's just a matter of finding the correct law and a decent argument. Provided we can get you before a like-minded judge, it may be possible to challenge the decision to keep you incarcerated without any hope of release. Court decisions do not bring things to an end forever. They merely spur you on to further action. Nothing in this world is certain, save death and taxes. Ever since Caesar Augustus imposed an estate tax to pay for imperial Roman exploits, death and taxes have walked hand in bony hand. But your case may help to prove that only taxes are certain in this uncertain world.'

I wasn't at all sure what he meant by his last remark but I understood that he was proposing that there might be a legal way of challenging my continued imprisonment. It didn't make much sense so I dived in with both feet.

'Why are you interested in my case?' I asked. 'David tells me you're the most highly paid and successful libel lawyer in the country. Why would you risk your reputation on a case you believe to be hopeless yourself? It makes no sense to me. Your normal clients are wealthy celebrities and politicians who apparently become emotionally distraught and have their reputations ruined because a newspaper calls them boring or they're caught with their fingers in the till and can't face up to their responsibilities. People like me fought for those bastards. Frankly, they make me sick. Sure, after all the hullabaloo of a high profile court case, all that happens in the end is that some of their wealth is transferred to you and within a couple of weeks everybody has forgotten all about it. Nobody dies, nobody goes to prison and nobody is locked up in a mental institution. Self-indulgent bastards if you ask me. Why would you want to get involved in a case like mine, with all those easy pickings out there?'

He appeared unaffected by my outburst and rose from his seat, indicating to the nurse that he was leaving.

'Let's just say I get bored easily,' he responded in answer to my question. I was surprised when he offered his hand.

'I'll be in touch. David has other things to discuss with you so I'll take my leave for now. Goodbye.'

He turned to David. 'I'll be outside in the car. There's no rush, I have some notes to dictate so take as long as you need.'

With that he headed for the door and I watched in silence as the nurse unlocked the doors allowing him to leave. As the door closed behind him, I wondered if I'd ever follow in his footsteps into the world outside.

'George! George!'

David's voice roused me from my thoughts.

'Sorry,' I said, 'I was somewhere else. It's been quite a morning. How did you manage to obtain the birth and marriage certificates?'

'It's a simple process, nowadays,' he said. 'In fact, you can do it over the Internet using the Family Records Office. The army records were a bit more difficult to obtain but the Freedom of Information Act helped. Service records before 1923 are kept in the National Archives, but those after that date are with the Ministry of Defence and getting anything out of them isn't easy.'

'Service records?' I said, astonished. 'Are you saying you got access to my service records?'

'That's right. Pay, pension, musters, medals, operational files and some other stuff. They support everything you've told me about your army career. All of it, national service, basic training, the Italian campaign. Everything from the day you first joined up.'

This was incredible news and I felt exhilarated. Surely this would help me prove who I really was? My mind was full of questions but I couldn't decide which one to ask first until I finally blurted out:

'When did I leave the army?' My thinking was if I knew the answer to that, it may explain some of this nightmare. 'Do my records say when I left the army?'

David looked sombre and thoughtful. He glanced over at the nurse, who was preoccupied with another patient that was feeling distressed. He swiftly withdrew a small hip flask from his inside jacket pocket and poured some of the amber liquid into my empty teacup.

'Drink that,' he said. 'You'll need it.'

I drank it down in one swallow and felt the smooth taste of a good malt whisky. A warm glow rose in my stomach and I felt my cheeks flush.

'That's a fine malt,' I said, savouring the taste all over again. 'So what have you to tell me. When did I get demobbed?'

My question seemed to sadden him and he sat silently for what seemed a long time before he spoke.

'You never did,' he said. 'You never did ... your army records reveal that you died on active service in Italy on 17th July, 1945. The same day that little Pietro Hunter was born.'

I heard him clearly, but I couldn't respond. This was too incredible to take in. How in the name of anything that bordered on sanity could I have died fifty-five years ago and still be seated here in a mental hospital very much alive. The only explanation was that I was indeed quite mad.

'I give up,' I said. 'I have no answer to this. It's madness. Either I'm living some sort of dream or I'm surrounded by lunatics.'

At this point I rose from my seat and indicated to the nurse that I wanted to go back to my room.

'Ten minutes,' David said, as I rose from the chair. 'Give me ten minutes. If I haven't convinced you by then we'll forget the whole thing. Father Flaherty trusted you, I trust you, Paul trusts you. When are you going to learn to trust us?'

I sat back down again and waved the nurse away.

'Ten minutes,' I said, and settled back down in my chair. I noticed David looked pensive and seemed to be having difficulty knowing where to begin.

'I've been a journalist for a long time,' he began. 'I didn't come into the job as a cynic. I suppose I thought I could make a difference. Naivety is a wonderful quality, but it doesn't last long in this business. Very early on you learn that most of the people you meet are trying to use you in one way or another. Of course, the more of a reputation you develop, the more useful you may become, so they feed you bullshit and you spend a lot of the time trying to establish what they're really getting at. Politicians, businessmen, lawyers, press officers, celebrities, sportsmen, agents, business managers – you name it. They see journalists as a means of getting what they want. But that's the name of the game and once you understand that it's easy enough to play along. Naturally, you become cynical about almost everything. There's an old saying that the higher up the tree the monkey goes the more you see of its arse and I've seen quite a few arses in my day. So, I suppose what I'm saying is I'm a cynical old bastard with a specific view on most things in

144

the world. I don't believe anything a politician tells me, I have no religion or any of that other shit. When you're dead *you're* dead and that's an end of the matter as far as I'm concerned. I don't know why we're here and I care even less. To me, the only philosopher I can remember who spoke any sense was Hobbes who said man's life is nasty, brutish and short. At least that's how I used to think, until I met you.'

'So what's happened?' I asked.

'You! You're what happened. Who the hell are you? You're not Peter Hunter, I know that. You can't be George Giles, he's been dead for over fifty years, the evidence is overwhelming.'

'What evidence?'

'For the past few months I've ploughed through more records than I care to remember. I've traced the Giles family back over one hundred and fifty years. The army records I've looked at prove that the George Giles you claim to be, died on the 17th July 1945, along with three of his comrades. It was a landmine that got them. The field was supposed to have been swept for mines but it had been missed, so there was an enquiry at which over a dozen witnesses gave evidence and all of them knew the four men well. They were their comrades in arms, if you like. There's no case of mistaken identity, none whatever. In fact, one of the witnesses was their commanding officer.'

'Captain Akehurst,' I said. 'I've suddenly remembered his name. Captain Akehurst! He was a real nice bloke. Firm but fair. He was a northerner. Came from Blackpool, I believe. The men liked him.'

'How could you know that?' he asked, perplexed. 'How could you know his name? I checked with the army and the files on this case haven't been accessed by anyone for over fifty years. If anyone had researched them, it would have been noted. The army doesn't let just anybody access their data. So, how can you know so much about George Giles? That's the question I keep asking myself, but any answer I come up with is anathema. I tell myself that it isn't possible that someone can come back from the dead, but in your case I can find no other logical explanation.'

David was clearly very frustrated and I understood why. I supposed that for the first time in his life, he was faced with something he couldn't explain rationally and was being drawn beyond the barriers of his mind to think the unthinkable. His lack of religious beliefs and his philosophy of never believing anything that he couldn't prove were being tested to the utmost. However, many things in the world cannot be proven, but we learn to take them for granted. We may know how the mechanics of the universe work but we don't know why it exists at all: we simply accept that it does. We understand natural law, mathematics and other phenomenon in terms of how they function but our collective wisdom has not yet figured out why. Hundreds of years of philosophy, theology, physics, and other disciplines have never been able to explain why we are here and probably never will.

As far as I was concerned, the facts may say I died in 1945; the reality was I was very much alive and sitting here with David in the year 2000. If I was dead, he must also be dead. On the other hand, perhaps all I was experiencing was happening inside my head. Perhaps none of these people existed but in my mind. Maybe I was simply in the middle of a vivid dream and would awaken in 1945 and remember nothing. Meanwhile, I had to play the role I appeared to have been assigned.

'Listen, David,' I said, 'I'm George Giles and that is a fact. I don't need proof to know who I am. The rest of you may, but I don't. Everything I experience, I experience as George Giles. All of my childhood memories, my family, friends, army buddies, jobs, everything tells me that's who I am, in the exact same way that everything you experience tells you that you are David McIntosh. Can you imagine what it would be like if all of a sudden the whole world began to tell you were someone else? That who you believe you are is nothing but a figment of your imagination. That you're suffering from a condition known as multiple personality disorder. That you're simply a trick of your own mind. That your mind has created another person to permit you to escape from the horror of who you really are. I am who I say I am. I'm not Peter Hunter the psychopathic killer. I can't explain where I've been for the last half-century – I simply don't know.'

I took a deep breath before continuing.

'I was walking down a road in Italy with three of my army buddies. It was July 1945, and we took a short cut across a field. That's the last thing I remember before waking up in the hospital fifty-five years later with another man's face. You know the rest and I know my past but my future is another matter. The way I see it, I've probably got another ten years or so left. What's the difference if I spend them in here or out there? I'd probably struggle to cope with the outside world anyway. I've been here for months, I've got warmth, shelter, three square meals a day, access to books and writing materials. I'm even studying for a degree. I've made some friends among the patients and staff and I'm reasonably content. So why don't you forget all about me. If you live for another hundred years, you'll still not get to the bottom of this. How can a dead man resurface after fifty odd years in the body of another man? You won't get an answer to that.'

David had watched me fixedly and now decided to intervene.

'Paul might,' he said. 'He's a clever guy. We've discussed

your case at length and I know he has some ideas.'

'Ideas? What sort of ideas?' I asked.

'He won't say, but that's not unusual for Paul. He always plays things close to his chest.'

'What's his interest? He never quite got round to explaining that earlier.'

'As I said, he believes in human rights. The individual has the right to life, liberty and the pursuit of happiness, as the Americans say. Staying with the Americans, he comes from a school of lawyers who believe in the philosophy of a black civil rights lawyer that a lawyer is either a social engineer or a parasite on society. He's chosen a bit of both. He's parasitic as a libel lawyer for the famous and he's made a fortune from their vanity. On the other hand, he's an altruistic social engineer; particularly in the charitable work he's done for the advancement of human rights. Frankly, although he's a very well-respected member of the bar, there's a bit of an anarchist lurking under the surface. He simply loves having a go at the State. To him, the individual is more important than any collection of politicians or government. That's why he agreed to get involved in your case, if you'll let him.'

'In what way? How can he get involved? Even if he could get the case into court, how could he possibly convince a judge or jury that I'm someone called George Giles, who died in 1945? Every doctor who's ever looked at my case will swear I'm Peter Hunter and I have a mental illness or psychological problem that leads me to deny who I really am. They'll say I'm a modern-day Jekyll and Hyde. Dr Jekyll is who you see now, but at anytime I could become Mr Hyde. I'm too dangerous to ever be released. That's what they'll say.'

David rose from his chair.

'I think my ten minutes are up,' he said. 'If you want Paul's help then I suggest you keep your head down and proceed as you are doing. If you want to remain here for the rest of your natural life, tell me now and that'll be an end of the matter. You have one minute before I leave.'

'Suppose I agree,' I said. 'What's in it for me?'

'The potential to be a free man. The right to walk along a beach on a winter's morning with a dog and hear nothing but the roars of the white horses and the gulls overhead.'

'And Paul, what's in it for him?'

'The opportunity to do what he enjoys most, I suppose. Pitting his wits against the establishment. He likes nothing better than a good argument.'

'And you?'

'Me? Well I get the exclusive rights to your story, a book deal I suppose, and a whole bunch of money. I get the wealth, Paul gets the honour, but you, you get the biggest prize of all. You get your freedom. Your minute is up. What's it to be?'

'Let's go for it,' I said, 'I have nothing to lose.'

CHAPTER EIGHTEEN

It was over six months since I'd agreed to accept the offer of help from Paul Thornton. He had said it would probably take sometime before I heard anything, but I didn't expect it to be half a year. I'd had some correspondence from both men but basically it was business documents that I was required to sign: a contract from David's agent granting him exclusive rights to anything he wrote about my life and some legal documents from Paul, mostly relating to applications for financial help to fund the case. I must admit that when I signed them I thought it was quite an amusing position to be in. Most people thought I was insane and if indeed I was mad, my signatures probably wouldn't be accepted by the law anyway, but nonetheless I signed and waited for Paul or David to get in touch, but apart from the written correspondence I hadn't had any contact with either man since I returned the signed documents.

During that time, I tried not to think about the case and took things as they came, one day at a time. My studies kept me busy in the evenings, and during the day, when the weather permitted, I worked in the gardens and if the rains came, I helped out in the hospital library. Considering I was confined in a hospital for the criminally insane, my life was peaceful and relatively uncomplicated. There was the odd confrontation between some patients and a member of staff, but these were generally brought under control quite quickly. In fact, I often thought that my life was much like that of a gardener who tended a large estate. Of course, I couldn't walk down to the village pub on a warm summer's evening for a beer, but apart from that there were many similarities. In any event, it was a better life than some of the troops I'd met just after the war ended and who had been incarcerated by the Germans in some godforsaken prisoner-of-war camp for two or three years. They'd managed to survive and keep their spirits up and I told myself I could do likewise.

I still met regularly with the doctors, answered their questions as best I could, took part in their tests and generally co-operated, apart from insisting I wasn't Peter Hunter and sticking to my belief that I was George Giles. It appeared that we were at a stalemate on that single matter, and I began to think I was just edging things a little, when some of them took to calling me George.

It was following one of the monthly review meetings, as I was making my way back to the library, when I was surprised to be told by a nurse that David was in the visiting hall. Although I hadn't thought much about when, if ever, I'd see him again, I was suddenly gripped by a feeling of anticipation and began to hurry along the corridor, eager to meet him.

When I entered the hall I saw him sitting alone at a table next to the tea-bar. He rose from his seat when he saw me approach and hurried towards me. He shook my hand warmly, put his left hand on my shoulder and urged me towards the table.

'Christ! You're looking great!' he exclaimed as we sat down. 'What do they feed you in here?'

'The food is all right,' I said. 'I watch what I eat and keep myself fit. Not like some I could mention.'

The reference to him having put on some weight since we last met wasn't missed and he patted his stomach.

'Too much high living,' he said, laughing. 'Paid for by the taxpayer, of course. You know, junkets, dinner parties, that sort of thing. All legitimate expenses arising in the course of one's duty.'

'Still as cynical as ever.' I said. He looked quite solemn, I thought, before he answered.

'Well maybe! Maybe! Anyway, I have some good news for you.'

Again, I was struck with a feeling of anticipation. 'What news?' I asked, unable to hide my excitement.

'Paul's managed it.'

'Managed what?'

'Managed to get you a hearing. A review of your case.'

Suddenly my heart sank and the excitement vanished. My case had been reviewed over and over again. A review was a foregone conclusion. You sat in front of a panel of doctors, social workers, probation officers and the like. All of them asked questions and in the end made the decision they'd come armed with before you'd answered one of them. It was farcical and I suddenly felt everything had been a waste of time and I should never have agreed to Paul taking on my case.

'What's wrong?' David asked. 'You look deflated. I thought you'd be pleased that things are moving forward.'

'I'm sorry,' I said, 'but these reviews are meaningless. The decisions are made before the event. There's no independent thought: just a bunch of doctors, social workers, probation staff, and mental health workers. They're all part of the State structure in one way or another and none of them are going to rock any boats. It's of no earthly use.'

David looked at me and smiled. 'It's not a case review here in the hospital. You misunderstood, or I didn't make it clear enough. It's a legal remedy – a judicial review or something along those lines it's called. It takes place in the High Court, in front of a judge. The judge has the power to question the actions of the public body concerned. Evidence is taken from witnesses on both sides. It's a proper, independent, legal process. Not an administrative procedure like you've just explained. You'll be legally represented by Paul and his legal team.'

I sat, unable to speak for a few moments. This was different and although I felt a slight tinge of hope, it was tempered by some doubt about the sort of argument that would be needed to persuade a High Court judge to order the release of someone the newspapers had dubbed the most dangerous man in Britain.

'So, what happens next?' I asked, when I found my voice.

'Paul will begin submitting the papers and prepare the procedural stuff,' he said. 'These will be served on the hospital authorities and I expect they'll shuffle them straight off to their lawyers. Incidentally, when the hospital becomes aware you're launching a legal challenge, I suppose you'll be asked to take part in a number of tests, but nothing that you haven't been through before, although I expect they'll be more thorough and involved. You'll probably be put under covert hour watch in order that they can gather any sort of information to support their arguments. They'll no doubt be looking for any signs of violent behaviour. Frankly, I wouldn't be surprised if they tried to goad you into behaving badly, so be on your guard.'

What David was saying was interesting but I didn't really believe anyone would go as far as to try and push me into losing my temper, but I would be prepared for it if they did. Besides, my army training had fitted me up to deal with such matters so I felt confident that I could pass any test they threw at me, but I had some other concerns.

'You said the review would be in front of a judge. Will there be witnesses?' I asked and David seemed a little hesitant before he answered.

'Paul will be calling witnesses as far as I know,' he replied.

This was quite unsettling. 'What witnesses could he call on my behalf?' I thought. Everybody I'd known in this world had long departed it.

'Everyone I used to know is now dead,' I said, but as if he hadn't heard me, David told me that Paul wanted to speak with the medium I'd met in Glasgow and asked for her name and address.

'Jean Robinson, I think,' I said, 'It was in a spiritualist hall in Berkeley Street. I can't remember exactly what the name of the church was. Why does he want her details?' Again he ignored my question.

'That'll do,' he said, 'I'll be in Glasgow next week at my flat and I'll sort it out then. Oh! And there's one other thing. Paul asked me if you are Catholic and whether you believe in God. To be honest, I'd no idea. Are you and do you?'

'I am and I do,' I answered, puzzled. 'Why does he want to contact this medium and why is he interested in my religious beliefs?'

'I have no idea and when it comes to Paul – I'd rather not try to speculate why he asks or does anything. I expect she is one of the witnesses he wants to call on your behalf, but that's only my guess. What your religion has to do with it is anybody's guess.'

'Witness!' I cried out disbelievingly. 'A medium! If that's the best he can come up with I don't hold out much hope. Hardly anyone takes these people seriously. What the hell is she likely to be a witness to, in my case?'

'Paul generally knows what he's doing,' David said quite

calmly. 'I wouldn't worry. You'll just have to learn to trust him. From what he's told me he intends to challenge the right of the authority to keep you locked up on the ground that you are insane. Peter Hunter was clearly mad, but George Giles clearly isn't. Not if we accept all the test results. He's basing some sort of argument around the M'Naghten rules.'

'M'Naghten rules? What are they?'

'It's a legal precedent from the 1800s. A guy called Daniel M'Naghten, a Scotsman like myself, began to believe he was a victim of a conspiracy, involving the Pope and the British Prime Minister. Sometime around 1840 he told various people, including the police and a Member of Parliament, that he was being persecuted by the Tories and Prime Minister Robert Peel, in particular. After stalking Peel for days in London he saw a man he thought was the prime minister and shot him in the back. The victim was in fact Peel's secretary, Edward Drummond, who died several days later. The case produced the rules that are now used to establish whether someone is insane and therefore unable to stand trial. If a person cannot be said to have understood the nature of their crime or is not capable of instructing a lawyer in their defence, then the courts rule they are insane. The rules establish insanity in a legal sense rather than a medical way. Basically, the rules are guidelines laid down by the House of Lords. If the criteria are satisfied, a special verdict of 'not guilty by reason of insanity' is delivered and the sentence is a mandatory and indeterminate period of treatment in a secure hospital facility. At least, that's what happens in England, other countries may take a different approach. Mostly it's legal mumbo jumbo to me, but the rules have stood the test for over one hundred and fifty years. Anyway, it wouldn't be seen as socially acceptable nowadays to punish the mentally ill for doing something they didn't know was wrong.'

'So what happened to M'Naghten?'

David looked as if he didn't want to answer but I pressed him.

'He died, here in Broadmoor, twenty odd years after he was found to be insane. Anyway, that was a long time ago. Paul's also likely to challenge the right to keep you locked up, on the grounds that you are no longer receiving any form of treatment. You display no propensity to violence and you are not mentally ill in the sense that medication is given to control your behaviour. Apparently, if you cannot be treated, there may be a legal loophole that could force your release but I wouldn't rely on this too much, as Paul thinks the government will move to close it soon and make any new law retrospective. At the moment, he reckons about eight murderers in institutions around the country may apply to be released on the grounds that they cannot be treated for their disorder and they are no longer insane. It's a legal minefield, but I wouldn't rely on this argument a whole lot.'

'What about the first point?' I asked. 'The fact that as George Giles I'm perfectly sane.'

'There's probably more chance with that but as you've said they think you're some sort of Jekyll and Hyde. So they'll probably argue that although Jekyll may be sane, Hyde certainly isn't.'

'Doesn't sound too promising from where I'm sitting,' I said. 'If that's it, I don't think I have much of a chance.'

'That won't be it if I know Paul – and I do. I'm sure he'll have something more up his sleeve.'

'Have you any idea what it may be?'

'Not really, but there's definitely something on his mind. I was going through some material with him the other evening.

Stuff about your case, mainly. My research into the Giles family tree, your war record, army files, that sort of thing. Whilst I was doing this, I came across a provisional witness list he's put together. It made quite peculiar reading.'

'Peculiar. In what way peculiar?'

'I'm not that sure, but when I examined it I noticed that the witnesses who may appear for the hospital are all ... I suppose you could say scientists of one sort or another. Doctors, psychiatrists, psychologists, forensic experts, geneticists, those kind of guys. On the other hand, all of the witnesses he's considering calling on your behalf are ...' he hesitated a little.

'Well ... thinkers, I suppose you'd say: philosophers, theologians, and the like, and of course the medium you met in Glasgow. It's like religion versus science. Quite paradoxical, really, as Paul himself is a devout atheist, if I can put it like that. So whatever he has in mind, it's difficult to figure out and he won't say, but no doubt it'll be interesting.'

I wasn't sure that interesting was the word I would have chosen, but I let it pass and simply asked if he knew when the case would come to court.

'It's hard to say,' was his reply. 'It depends a great deal on how the lawyers for the hospital play it when the papers are served. They'll probably start the legal game early on in the process and delay things under mountains of paperwork and legal wrangling about what is and isn't admissible, requests for more time, adjournments, that sort of stuff. It could be months, maybe longer, so you'll have to be patient and watch what you do. The hospital would love you to start acting as if you are insane. So be prepared. Meanwhile, if there's anything you need give me a call, I presume you're allowed the use of a phone now?'

157

'Within limits, but everything is taped.'

'In that case, don't discuss anything about the case over the phone. If Paul needs to see you, he'll come here or I'll come along in his place.'

For the next half hour or so we sat chatting about things other than the forthcoming legal issues. It seemed pointless to speculate any further on what was likely to happen and the court case was a long way off. I imagined that the lawyers would try all sorts of tactics and legal manoeuvring and it could be as much as a year or more before anything practical took place. Mostly we chatted about my life within the hospital and I told him about the inmates who'd become my new friends and how we got through each day.

There was Frank Delaney, who, twenty years earlier had murdered his wife and mother-in-law with an axe. He was driven to this act of violence when, after only a few months of marriage, he learned that his young wife was having an affair with a former school friend. So he armed himself with a woodcutter's axe and bludgeoned her to death. He meted out the same treatment to her mother when he discovered she had been aware of the affair and didn't tell him. At his trial his defence successfully argued that he was insane and he was incarcerated for life. Over the last twenty years, he had responded well to treatment and was now being considered for a move to an open hospital with a view to releasing him back into the community. It was almost impossible to believe that this small, bespectacled, rather nervous, balding, fifty-five year-old man could ever have been the crazed axe murderer that the newspapers dubbed him. Now, he was the hospital postman and my chess partner.

Then there was another friend: Althea Elaine Constans Spencer. A girl as beautiful as the Greek goddesses she was named after. Thea, as she was known, was forced by her family to have an abortion when she was only fourteen years-old and had fallen pregnant to an older man. At eighteen, she became a nurse and now at twenty-seven, was facing the rest of her life in Broadmoor after being held unfit to stand trial for the killing of seven children in her care. It was never established what drove her to commit these acts and she never spoke about them. Most of the time, she was in total denial and when she was having a really bad day, she'd stand by the wall of the hospital near the large gates, waiting for her father to come and take her home. He never came, of course, and at night you could hear her sobbing herself to sleep. At other times, she appeared very rational and was quite a personable young girl, but underneath she was extremely disturbed.

Henry Mair was a thirty-four year-old man entering his ninth year in Broadmoor. Tragically, he lost his young wife to a rare form of cancer leaving him with three small children and no visible means of support. One winter's evening, in a fit of absolute despair, he drove the children to a quiet spot where he used to visit and sit with his young wife on balmy summer evenings. He gave the children some hot chocolate laced with sleeping pills and when they'd fallen asleep, he attached a hosepipe to the car exhaust and fed it into the interior through the boot. He drank from a bottle of wine as he sat writing a suicide note before he became unconscious. As often happens, fate took a hand and another motorist, who'd stopped to relieve himself, spotted the car. It was too late to save the children but Henry was revived and rushed to hospital where he recovered. He was also found unfit to stand trial and committed to Broadmoor under a hospital order. The drugs and talking therapies had helped him regain his sanity but the price was living with almost unbearable feelings of remorse, which required further treatment. These patients and others

159

had all committed horrific crimes, but none of them seemed especially dangerous to me and, if anything, I felt that they were to some extent victims themselves, but that wasn't how the authorities or the public saw them. There were, of course, some patients who were indeed very dangerous individuals, but they were detained in another part of the hospital and under constant supervision. Henry and Frank now accepted responsibility for what they'd done and were truly remorseful, but Thea had blocked all memory of her actions and it was unlikely that she would ever be released. It was almost certain that a number of the other patients would never see the outside world again, in particular a former civil servant who'd killed fifteen young men and disposed of their body parts in drains and sewers around the city of London. The detective who had interviewed him about the killings said that at his trial he appeared relaxed, cooperative and matter of fact but he didn't show any signs of remorse and it was as though he was talking about someone else.

These were my new friends, for how long I could only guess. Some of them would move on as time went by but despite David's optimism I felt it was more than likely that I would probably spend the rest of my life confined among this group of murderers and maniacs.

'Why don't you write about them,' David said, in a matter-of-fact way. 'You're gaining an insight into mental disorders that few people ever will. They trust you, I've noticed that.'

'That's because they see me as one of them. I'm a serial killer, remember? At least that's what everyone believes. Besides, I don't see the point.'

'It would give you some purpose, perhaps. It may help some of us understand what evil really is and why some people do what they do. Just a thought. I'll leave it with you.'

He might as well not have bothered as I'd already dismissed the idea from my mind, preferring to turn my thoughts and energies to the forthcoming court case.

CHAPTER NINETEEN

The Royal Courts of Justice, or the Old Bailey as it is better known, is a grey stone, Victorian Gothic building that sits on the Strand in London. As a child growing up in the city, I'd passed the imposing structure many times, but today would be the first time I'd get the chance to see it from the inside. It had been seven months since David had first told me that Paul had succeeded in getting my case into court and here we were at last. It would have been interesting to enter the building under its large archway like a free person, but I had to settle for being driven in the back of a heavily guarded police van through a side door. When the van pulled abruptly to a halt, I was escorted into a cell by four armed police officers. Within a few minutes of my arrival, Paul Thornton was shown into the cell and I almost didn't recognise him in his court robes and horsehair wig. When the door was locked behind him, he looked me straight in the eye with his now familiar piercing gaze.

'Good morning,' he said cheerily before turning to one of the officers and handing him a piece of paper. Upon reading it, the officer shrugged offhandedly, removed my handcuffs and indicated to the other officers that they should vacate the cell. When they were gone, Paul produced a packet of cigarettes and, after lighting one for himself, handed me the packet and an expensive gold cigarette lighter.

'You can keep the cigarettes but I want the lighter back,' he said, smiling. He turned his back on me and looked up at the small, rectangular window placed high up on the cell wall and began to speak:

'I never saw a man who looked

With such a wistful eye

Upon that little tent of blue

Which prisoners call the sky

And at every drifting cloud that went

With sails of silver by.'

He paused, then explained. 'Oscar Wilde, *The Ballad of Reading Gaol*. I think of it every time I visit this cell and see that small rectangle of blue sky that Wilde spoke so eloquently about. He was perhaps the greatest poet that Ireland ever produced, and we threw him into prison and broke his spirit simply because he was different. A stain on the British justice system and unfortunately, not the only one. History is littered with miscarriages of justice. Let's hope that this case does not prove to be another one.'

Quite suddenly, his contemplative mood changed and he became the professional lawyer.

'This case will depend much on how arguments develop during the hearing,' he said. 'I don't expect you will understand much of what is said today as there are a number of points of law being raised. Others have been settled and I'll run through them briefly with you now. Firstly, the case will now be heard by a judge and jury. The judge has accepted a legal submission that if the onus is on a defender to prove he is insane, which is the present law, then justice demands that if the State wishes to keep the defender incarcerated on the grounds of insanity, then it is up to the State to prove he remains insane. This simply means that the state will present their evidence first. It has also been agreed that you will sit at the table alongside our legal team and I. You are not on trial here. Finally, I have not yet decided whether you should give evidence – that will very much depend on how things develop. Now, have you any questions?'

It was all a bit much for me and I couldn't think of anything to ask so I simply shook my head.

'Good!' he said, 'I'll see you upstairs shortly,' and with that he rattled the cell door, which almost instantly swung open noisily to let him out.

Fifteen or so minutes later, I was shown into the body of the court by four police officers and escorted to the table at which Paul sat with two other bewigged lawyers, one male and one female. I took a seat beside him and noticed that the officers sat immediately behind me.

The table was piled high with files containing witness statements, law books and, I noticed, a number of books on different religions and philosophies, and I concluded if these were to be consulted at any length the case was likely to go on for a long time. The room was filled to capacity and there was a great deal of murmuring, movement and whispered conversations among court officials and the spectators, who I imagined were mostly journalists. Suddenly, a voice rang out ordering the court to stand and as we rose to our feet, the judge appeared, took his place on the bench, nodded politely to the assembled court, and indicated we should be seated. As we sat down I whispered to Paul, asking why the jury box was empty.

'There are some legal points being raised by the government,' he said. 'These will be heard in the jury's absence. Relax, it'll be a long day.'

His words proved prophetic and for the rest of the day I sat and listened as one legal argument after another ensued and the judge ruled for one side or the other. By late afternoon there was still no sign of the jury and the proceedings were drawn to a close around four o'clock when I was escorted back to my cell before being driven back to Broadmoor.

It was not until the following afternoon that the jury appeared, indicating that the legal points had been settled and the hearing proper was about to begin. I studied the twelve men and women closely as they filed into the jury box. The seven men and five women spanned quite a broad age group from late twenties to late sixties, and clearly represented different cultures and religions. What I saw was a mixture of age, culture and experience, which gave me some heart as the first witness was called.

Over the next three days the government called a steady stream of expert witnesses, around twelve in all. One by one the doctors, psychiatrists, psychologists, and forensic experts entered the witness box and piece by damning piece they built up a profile of Peter Hunter and his decline into madness. As a child he'd been subjected to some tragic events, they said, including the loss of the only two people in the world who cared about him, his father and grandmother. Alone and being cared for by the State, he created his own fantasy world in which he was in control of everything and everybody. He was a quiet child, who never made friends easily and seemed happiest left to his own devices. Those who had responsibility for his care seemed happy to let him develop at his own pace. According to some of the witnesses, Hunter could have developed a mental illness by the time he was about twelve years old, and without treatment it had become progressively worse, so that by the age of eighteen he was a paranoid schizophrenic. He was cunning, highly intelligent and manipulative, but in their view quite mad and very dangerous. Hunter, they said, believed he'd been chosen by God for a mission to rid the world of women he perceived as evil. So by the time he was thirty, he'd committed his first murder. Other murders followed until he was eventually caught and brought before the courts. Although he was found fit to stand trial, he was later held to be insane and moved from a secure prison to Broadmoor hospital. From my position, most of the experts were agreed on Hunter's mental state, save when it came to the point about whether he was suffering from a condition known as multiple personality disorder. Some of the experts believed he was and others felt he might be faking the condition in order to obtain an early release.

Dr Robert Phelps, a forensic psychiatrist, testified that Hunter did in fact suffer from multiple personality disorder, or dissociative identity disorder as others called it. He explained that the condition was generally due to trauma suffered during childhood. Memory and other aspects of consciousness, he explained, were divided up among the different "alters" or personalities, and amnesia was a symptom of the condition. This could explain why Hunter's "alter", George Giles, had no recollection of Hunter's crimes or his past life. Whilst he agreed that there was no real consensus among experts as to what an "alter" actually was, he proposed that there was a general acceptance that the cause is repressed memories of childhood sexual abuse. But others had stated there was no evidence that Hunter had ever suffered that type of abuse as a child. Multiple personality disorder was clearly a complex phenomenon, with some witnesses believing it was nothing more than a creation of therapists and others that it was a real condition where sufferers created a boundary so that the horror doesn't happen to them, doesn't happen at all or happens to some other self.

'Was this what I was doing?' I asked myself. 'Was I really Peter Hunter and had I created another self in order to escape the horrors of my past?' I had no sooner had this frightening thought when one of the witnesses began to talk about an

American case where a strangler was defended on the ground that it was his other personality who committed the murders and not he. According to the witness, the prosecution successfully argued that the defence was a sham. 'If that happened here I would be returning to Broadmoor for the rest of my life,' I thought. By late afternoon I had convinced myself that the case was going nowhere and I'd never be a free man again, unless I made good an escape. It was not a great start to the weekend.

When the court reconvened after the weekend break, the prosecution called their final witness – Dr Wilson. His evidence was short and along much the same lines as the others. In his view, it didn't matter whether I was suffering from a personality disorder or not. What mattered was whether I remained as my "alter" George Giles, or whether Hunter returned. In his view, the risk of this happening was too great and therefore I wasn't fit to be released and could still be considered as a danger to the public. When he was finished his evidence, the judge asked my defence team if they had any questions. At that point, Paul Thornton rose to his feet.

'I do indeed, my Lord,' he said.

His response shook me wide-awake. This was the first time since the hearing began that he'd taken the opportunity to cross-examine any of the witnesses. On the eleven previous occasions he'd been asked the same question he'd politely declined. Although I was as far away from being an experienced court lawyer as anyone could be, his tactics, if that's what they were, confused me. I'd expected he would have taken the opportunity to test each witness, raise objections, challenge their theories, in fact all the things I thought lawyers did. Instead he and his legal team had sat silent through the three days of evidence simply taking notes and having whispered conversations between each other.

'It's rather late in the day,' the judge said, 'and I expect you will have more than one question to put to this witness ...'

'Indeed, my Lord,' Paul replied.

'Then I suggest we adjourn until tomorrow.'

'As your Lordship pleases.'

The judge raised his hand and gently tapped it on the bench. 'Court adjourned until ten tomorrow morning,' and with that proceedings ended for the day.

Within a few moments I was taken downstairs to await the transport that would ship me back to Broadmoor. 'Things aren't going well,' I thought, as I sat in the cells below the court and looked up at the little rectangle of blue visible through the small window. I heard the key turn in the lock and rose to meet my escort, but instead Paul was shown into the room and the door locked behind him.

'You look quite depressed,' he said. 'I take it you don't think things are going our way?'

'No, I don't,' I said. 'Do you?' but before he could answer I continued: 'All I've listened to over the past couple of weeks is a load of medical jargon, all of which has one simple aim: to keep me locked up for the rest of my life. So far, our side hasn't successfully challenged any of their evidence, nor have we put any real counter arguments and according to those files and books on the desk our defence seems to be a mountain of religious mumbo jumbo. More to the point, the jurors look as if they've made up their minds already.'

Paul had listened carefully to what I had to say and when he was sure I'd finished my rant he smiled.

'We're only halfway through the hearing, George,' he said in a quiet, self-confident manner. 'You let me worry about the jury. I want you in court tomorrow morning looking confident and positive. The State's finished its case but ours is just beginning. It's not over yet, far from it. Trust me.'

It wasn't so much a request as an order and he turned and rattled the door of the cell. When it opened, he gave me a smile and vanished through the door whistling *Tipperary*, an old army song I knew very well.

CHAPTER TWENTY

There was a buzz of expectation the next morning when Paul Thornton QC approached the witness box to begin his cross-examination of Dr Wilson. His first question was simple:

'Who is George Giles?' he asked.

Dr Wilson responded in a clear and confident manner. 'George Giles does not exist other than in the mind or, if you like, within the imagination of Peter Hunter.'

'When you say he exists only in the mind of Peter Hunter, do you mean he's an invention? Someone Hunter has created in the same way a child creates an imaginary friend? He's faking, in other words? It's all made up?'

'It's possible he could be faking, but again it's equally possible he could be suffering from some sort of dissociative identity disorder.'

'A multiple personality disorder, is that what you mean?'

'I'm not happy with that term, exactly. It is such a complex area of medicine and the term means different things to different people.'

'But the symptoms are basically more or less agreed among psychiatrists and psychologist, whether you call it multiple personality disorder or dissociative identity disorder, is that so?'

'As I said, I'm not happy with the former term. It's much like the tendency for some people to talk about schizophrenia, as meaning someone with a split personality, which is wholly inaccurate and has no real medical meaning.'

'I mentioned the symptoms. It is said that those who suffer from this sort of condition have an alter ego, another personality if you like, and that personality takes over. In fact, they become that other person. Is that broadly correct?'

'In laymen's terms, broadly speaking, yes.'

'Amnesia. Is that another symptom? Do the major studies of this phenomenon show unexplained amnesia is a common occurrence among sufferers? Indeed, so much so that the new personality remembers nothing about the old. They have no recollection of their former personality's early childhood, friends, places they lived. All of their history is blacked out. Is that correct?'

'In most cases, that is correct. They become that other person, the "alter", as it's been termed.'

'Why? Why do such people adopt another personality? Is it a form of mental illness, a means of escape, is it that they don't like themselves, are they lonely, do we know?'

'Most writings on the subject suggest it is caused by the individual having a severe traumatic experience in childhood. Generally some form of sexual abuse.'

'To your knowledge, was Peter Hunter sexually abused as a child?'

'I have no way of knowing whether he was or wasn't. It is not something he has ever discussed.'

'How long have you known him?'

'Since he became my patient, about fifteen years ago.'

'You've had many discussions with him during that time, I take it?'

'Hundreds.'

'I ask you again. Was Peter Hunter sexually abused as a child?'

'Not that I'm aware of. Probably not. There is no evidence or allegations that he was. It never arose as a matter of discussion during our meetings.'

'Really. As part of his treatment has he ever been subjected to hypnosis?'

'Not to my knowledge.'

'If he had been, you would know? Correct?'

'If it was during the last fifteen years, I would expect to have been advised of it. As I recall, hypnosis was excluded as a potential treatment. Peter Hunter is a paranoid schizophrenic who believes, among other things, that he speaks with God. He is not a suitable candidate for that sort of talking therapy.'

'Interesting that you use the term "talking therapy". Is it true that there are basically two schools of thought here? One says that multiple personality disorder is a genuine medical condition and can be found in people who have been traumatised in childhood. The other says it's nothing more than the invention of therapists. In effect, the very same therapists who through the use of hypnosis, implant false memories into patients, who then go on to believe they are someone else, or something that happened in their past that makes them what they are. Is that a fair summary of the position?'

'There are people who hold these opposing views. But it's much more complex than that.'

'Indeed! Indeed, it appears to be. But for argument's sake, if Peter Hunter doesn't fit in with either of these propositions, where did his "alter" George Giles come from?'

'It's difficult to say. Hunter is a highly intelligent and

manipulative person. He could be faking the whole thing. It's a possibility.'

'Is it probable?'

'Not in my opinion, but others may differ. I don't believe he's faking. I'm sure he has a genuinely held belief that he is someone called George Giles, but this is a creation of his own imagination, in my opinion.'

'No such person ever existed. Is that what you're saying?'

'It's unlikely he did.'

'What do you mean, unlikely? Surely either George Giles is a real person or he is not?'

'Many people who suffer from a psychiatric or psychological disorder claim to be other people. In some cases, they claim to be famous people from years gone past. Napoleon, Joan of Arc, Jesus and so on.'

'Could they indeed actually be that person? Napoleon, Joan of Arc or Jesus?'

'I'm sorry. Your question does not make sense.'

'Reincarnation or re-birth?'

'I'm not an expert of reincarnation. That's another field of expertise.'

'Indeed! But it's so closely related to the work you do, that I thought perhaps you had an opinion. You are aware that there are many studies that appear to show a person may have more than one life. Many young children, for example, have claimed to remember a past life. What do you think of the two thousand children who claim to have lived in another life? Are they all suffering from a psychiatric or psychological illness?

'Not necessarily. Some may have a mental disorder; some

may be faking it, others fantasising. It is not my field of expertise.'

'None of them were diagnosed with any mental condition. They were examined by psychiatrists and psychologists but even with over eighty forms of mental illness to pick from, these children were found to be perfectly normal apart from the fact that they could outline the events, people and places of another life. What do you say to that?'

'As I said. Reincarnation is not my province.'

'Do you subscribe to the materialist view that because science cannot explain it, it doesn't exist?'

'I haven't really thought about it to any great depth.'

'And having not thought about it, you nevertheless felt qualified to come here and attempt to debunk my client's claims?'

'I was asked …'

'Thank you, doctor. I have no more questions at this time.'

At this point Paul returned to the table, leaving a rather flustered and upset witness confused as to whether he should leave the witness box or remain where he was. Lord MacLean came to his rescue by asking the crown agents if they wished to re-examine the witness but they declined and the doctor was excused, to his clear relief.

After lunch, Paul called his first witness: Dr Imtiaz, an Asian philosopher and Hindu teacher. He was a small, bespectacled man and from where I was sitting I could hardly see him over the top of the witness box, but his voice carried around the room when he spoke and he delivered his answers in a clear, relaxed and confident way. The main thrust of his evidence was that death did not bring about the end of a person's life.

He believed in reincarnation and related much of its long history, claiming its origins to be in India and later adopted by many other eastern religions. When prompted, he stated that his belief was that people could have many lives before reaching a final resting place. Whether this place was called Heaven, Nirvana, Paradise or any of a hundred other names did not matter. It was, he said, possible that Peter Hunter could have been George Giles in another life. This produced a series of theatrical gestures from the government's legal team and whispered voices from the audience. When he finished his evidence, Paul resumed his seat and the main barrister for the government rose to cross-examine. Despite his attempts at ridicule, sarcasm, mockery and scorn he could not shift the witness from his position. Life after death, to Dr Imtiaz, was a fact. It did not have to be proven scientifically – it was a matter of belief. It was a matter of faith. After much fencing back and forth, it was clear that the government's agent was very frustrated.

'No more questions,' he said in an exasperated tone, which he overemphasised for the benefit of the jury.

In my view, he fared no better in his cross-examination of the rest of the witnesses Paul called, as one by one they entered the witness box. Eminent scholars from around the world, representing many different religions, gave evidence one after another. They mostly had different views on what happens after death but there appeared to be a general acceptance that death by itself did not bring about the end of life. Father Flaherty smiled at me as he gave his evidence and Reverend Jean Robinson fended off a sustained and rather childish attack on her character with a passionate and calmly delivered put-down of the examining lawyer.

'When all the forensic skills possessed by the police come up with nothing,' she said, 'then they come for me. When science has failed them, then they come for me. When they suspend their disbelief for a few moments, then they come for me.'

She was confident and crystal clear in her responses and as I watched her treat her attacker with disdain it became clear that she was a person whose conviction and commitment to her beliefs was total.

In all, it took over four days for Paul's witnesses to complete their evidence. If what I observed had been an academic debate, I would have felt confident that I was on the winning team. Paul's team had clearly out pointed the opposition in terms of the arguments. The psychiatrists, psychologists, neurologists, and forensic experts had appeared unable to agree on anything. None of them were prepared to say that Peter Hunter was faking, nor were they able to determine whether he suffered from some form of personality disorder. Despite the fact that their medical Bible defined over eighty mental illnesses, none of them could confidently be applied to George Giles. In fact, a few of them argued that multiple personality disorder didn't exist and that this and other similar disorders were the creation of therapists and others. On the other hand, what differences there were around the concept of reincarnation were negligible and the general consensus among theologians and others was that life after death was a fact. This wasn't some scientific thesis that needed proof: belief was all that was required. Faith, in the simple logic that the material world made no sense unless there was something beyond it. They were not shackled by the arrogance of scientists who opined that if they couldn't explain it, it didn't exist. But this wasn't a debating society. The jury were charged with making a decision on what would become of me for the rest of my life. I would be a free man, or remain in Broadmoor until I died. They would never re-open my case again after this, of that I was wholly convinced. This was my last chance for freedom, I thought, as I sat and waited for the closing speeches and the judge's summing up to the jury to begin. In the end, the jury had to decide whether I was Peter Hunter, a man who would kill if allowed back into society; or George Giles, a quiet, God-fearing person to whom causing his neighbour an injury was anathema. There was no doubt in my mind that at this stage, the jury were unsure as to what way to go and like so many other court cases, much would depend on the closing speeches and the judge's final charge to the twelve men and women who held my fate in their hands.

CHAPTER TWENTY-ONE

The government counsel rose from his chair, adjusted his wig, tugged at his robe and approached the jury.

'Ladies and gentlemen,' he said, in a patronising tone. 'History will judge whether this case has any legal significance, or whether it is an affront to our system of justice. Peter Hunter, alias George Giles, is not on trial here. At least that's what my learned friend, the barrister for the defence, would have you believe. And he is quite right! This is not a trial – it is a review. Through a series of legal manoeuvrings, dogma, imaginary interpretations of laws that are hundreds of years-old, plausible argument, and his trademark jury perplexing style, my learned friend has managed to convince the court to hear what has turned into nothing more than a gathering of gibberish about life after death, reincarnation, religious canon and a whole host of other unproven ideas. Not one shred of solid, substantial proof from any quarter has been put before you. In law, this is a review, but that is not the reality. If you decide this man seated beside his lawyers is George Giles, he goes free. If you accept that he is Peter Hunter, he returns to a secure hospital. It is a trial in all but name.' It was a fierce opening and clearly he intended to continue in the same vein.

'The question you have to ask yourself, is whether you are prepared to risk freeing this man and putting the whole community at risk, on nothing more than the unsupported opinion of a group metaphysical poets with vivid imaginations. Hunter has been assessed by psychiatrists, psychologists and other medical professionals. Scientists who study the physical world. The world of pain. The sentient world. The real world. The world we, as human beings, recognise as bringing with it great joy, immense pain, happiness and wretchedness and in the end, death. To a man and a woman, these scientists agree that Peter Hunter is a dangerous psychopath regardless of what name he goes under. You have heard the forensic evidence that says his DNA and fingerprints are those of Peter Hunter, not George Giles.'

He paused and poured himself a drink of water from a carafe on the table. He looked over the top of the glass and eyed the jury.

'There is no George Giles! Hunter, in a botched attempt to escape from Broadmoor, fell from the hospital wall and was knocked unconscious. He was taken to a general hospital and after he recovered, he made good his escape. He was on the loose for a month, during which time he met some well-meaning, but naïve people whom he managed to convince he was someone else. Remember, the experts have testified that Hunter is an extremely intelligent person with a very high IQ, who is exceptionally cunning and manipulative. You have two questions to ask yourselves. Is Peter Hunter faking this other personality, hoping to convince you to release him back into the community?'

He went through the same process with the glass of water before turning to some of the other evidence.

'The experts tell us he was a very imaginative young child and as an adult, he certainly is capable of creating this elaborate hoax. His motive for doing so is very powerful – freedom. The other question you may consider, is whether Hunter is indeed suffering from a personality disorder and truly believes he is someone called George Giles. The theory here is that Mr Hyde is so traumatised by his past criminal actions that he has become Dr Jekyll, the good "alter" or good self. Good has triumphed over evil once more, but that triumph may be short-lived. There is no evidence to say that the "alter", Dr Jekyll, will remain and that Mr Hyde has gone forever. Were we to accept that he genuinely suffers from such a disorder, we must ask whether there is a risk in setting him free? The answer is yes! You must not set him free!'

He paused clearly for effect and a series of whispers and coughs were heard throughout the court. Satisfied with the response, he raised his voice ...

'The risk is too great. There are no other questions for you to ask yourselves. My learned friend has introduced you to a collection of theologists, philosophers, religious leaders, a priest and even one person who claims to speak with the dead. Their collective evidence amounts to no more than a short, potted history of some of the world's religions and philosophical theories. Not a single strand of real evidence. A fog, ladies and gentlemen. A smog as thick as pea soup. An elaborate smokescreen concocted by my learned friend to confuse, disorientate, perplex, baffle, bewitch and bewilder. Another tactic is to convince you, by means of selective documents, that George Giles was indeed a real person. That is most probably a fact, but the real George Giles is dead. His army records, introduced into evidence by the defence, tell us so. The man before you is an impostor. Do not be fooled and do not get lost in that fog. Send Hunter back to Broadmoor. That is where he belongs!'

It was almost noon when the counsel for the government sat down, and as he had done every other day, the judge adjourned for lunch and ordered us back at two in the afternoon.

Downstairs in the cold cell, I lunched on a greasy gammon steak and pineapple, overcooked chips and dried-out garden peas, washed down by a strong black tea with no sugar. Only Paul's speech and the judge's summing up were to come. After that, it was down to twelve individuals thrown together at random to make a decision. None of them had ever met before and it was unlikely they ever would again. People meet and form relationships under a variety of circumstances, at school, at work, in dance halls, at social events, in church, but I'd never heard anyone say they met the love of their life or their best friend serving on a jury. Charging ordinary people with the responsibility to send a fellow human being to prison for life, I supposed, was such an important event and for a short period of time overwhelmed them and forced them to concentrate on things other than themselves. But, it didn't matter what I supposed. All that mattered now was Paul's speech to these twelve people that he would make the following day. I toyed with my food as I thought through that morning's events, when I was suddenly aware I was floundering in the kind of fog described by the prosecuting counsel earlier.

CHAPTER TWENTY-TWO

I hadn't slept very well during the night and dozed in and out of slumber on my way to the court under my usual escort. I was still pretty drowsy when I was shown to my seat and I began to think it wasn't just the restless night I'd had, but I was experiencing the sort of fatigue that overcomes you when you feel all is lost.

'Good morning, George,' Paul said, smiling from ear to ear, when I arrived at the now familiar mahogany-coloured table in the courtroom. Before I could reply he continued speaking.

'We're coming round the last bend and there's one fence to jump and a gruelling two-furlong run in to the winning post. Do we try and get a quick breather into the horse or do we boot him in the belly and go hell for leather up the hill, knowing that victory can be snatched from our grasp at any time? This is the last fence. Let's get over it safely and hold on to him as long as we can.'

Before I could respond to his racing analogy, the jury entered and the court rose to its feet. With the judge and jury *in situ* Paul rose from his chair and approached the jury box with both hands clasped behind his back, under his robe. He walked silently back and forth in front of the twelve men and women, his head bowed as if in deep thought, before he raised it and began to speak.

'Ladies and gentlemen,' he said, smilingly politely at the jury. 'This is indeed a very unusual case, as my learned friend has said. But that, you will come to realise, is all he has said that I concur with. He presented two questions to ask yourselves. Firstly, is my client a crazed maniac who is fooling everybody by concocting a fake personality, so he can be free to continue his vendetta against women? Secondly, does he suffer from some form of personality disorder? My learned friend more or less told you what he believes. He believes George Giles to be an impostor. But let me deal with his second proposition first. From what you have heard from the Crown's witnesses, multiple personality disorder is not simple to define. In fact, some experts would rather use a different term altogether and, one could argue, that is because the existing term has become so discredited as to render it laughable. Assuming it existed at all, it is said to be induced in childhood, due to some traumatic event. Indeed, you may think it is strange that few, if any, children are troubled by this syndrome, as you've been told it only seems to manifest itself in adulthood and usually only after a visit to one of these so-called therapists. You've also heard that people may have many different personalities or perhaps just one other "alter", to use the jargon. Some say that the condition simply doesn't exist and is no more than an invention of therapists, chiefly those who may be taking vulnerable people and implanting the idea that they are someone else into their minds during their so called "healing sessions". Whilst this has not been satisfactorily proven, there is some circumstantial evidence, particularly of a kind that shows that a very large proportion of people who claim to be someone else, only ever do so after having spoken to a therapist. Charlatans and snake oil salesmen perhaps? That is a matter for you to consider. But remember, and remember well, when you retire to consider the future of my client, that all you have really heard from these so-called experts is theory and not, as they would have you believe, proven science. Science, it has been said, starts with a guess from which a hypothesis is developed, giving rise to a theory that requires proof. There is no firm proof that any such condition exists. Remember, also, that it has been held in this very place, as a matter of law, that the court has a duty to see that trial by judge and jury according to law is not subordinated by medical theories. So, you will remember it is your duty to reach a decision on the facts and not on medical theory.' Before he could continue, Lord MacLean interrupted.

'Counsel,' he said, sharply, 'if you are putting legal authority before the jury, I would have expected the court would have been made aware of it, if in fact it is an authority at all. But you propose it like it is.'

'It was a direct quote from "Young versus Young", my Lord. I believe it was your Lordship who wrote the decision.'

Lord MacLean did not betray his embarrassment at forgetting one of his own major decisions, but merely smiled and responded with confidence, 'Of course. But it was a long time ago.'

'Indeed my Lord, I was a law student at the time.'

'I didn't think it was quite that long ago, but I bow to your prodigious memory. You may proceed.'

The humour of the exchange did not go without notice and there were quite a few controlled sniggers around the courtroom. When they'd died down, Paul continued.

'Theory as I say, is not evidence. It is "ifs", "buts" and "maybes" and nothing more pretentious than that. In fact, that's why my learned friend, counsel for the government, prefers the fakery theory. He doesn't trust his own witnesses to have got it correct. As to the question of fakery, his argument is simple. My client has simply made everything up. In effect, he has created a new person called George Giles, just as a good author has us believe his characters really exist. Very plausible, simple to achieve, authors do it all the time. Dickens created the most memorable characters in all of literature I believe, but you cannot trace their genealogy, they don't have birth certificates, marriage certificates, army records and other documented proof of who they really are. George Giles has all of these, you have heard them discussed in evidence, and you have seen them with your own eyes. George Giles is a real person, not a creation. Did Peter Hunter invent all of this? How could he possibly have known anything about this ordinary man born in London in 1918? Hunter did not come into this world until 1945, another proven fact.'

I listened closely as Paul carried on with his speech and I began to think that he was indeed putting up a smokescreen. The jury looked confused as did the judge, but he was in full flow.

'As to the life and subsequent death and rebirth of my client,' he went on, 'I will get to those issues later. Meanwhile, I ask you to consider how Hunter could have gathered so many personal details about George Giles. It simply isn't possible. Some people may, as you have heard, claim to be Napoleon, but they cannot recount such intimate details of the man's life. They are simply acting out a fantasy. My client knows every minute detail about George Giles, just as each of you know your own self. It is that knowing that makes each of us who we are. That consciousness! George Giles has passed every test he has been subjected to. Observational assessments, IQ tests, psychological profiling and lie-detector tests. He has been examined by psychiatrists, neurologists, memory experts, amateur and professional, in the fields of science and medicine. They are all baffled. Every result says clearly and without equivocation he is a sane and rational human being. As sane and rational as any of us in this courtroom this morning. In other circumstances, it would be accepted without question that he is who he says he is. My learned friend's questions do not fit the facts. The real question for your consideration is, what happens after a person dies?'

This statement, in my view, did nothing to clear away the confusion but he pressed on, his voice booming around the court.

'For thousands of years, the greatest minds in the world have wrestled with the question. As of today, no one has come up with a definitive answer. Does death bring about finality to a man's life or does he live on in some other form? Does Reverend Jean Robinson really talk with dead people? Her evidence was very convincing, especially when she related the story about the young man who disappeared in Glasgow and turned out to have drowned in an accident on the river Clyde. She led the police to the very spot. The police, with all their resources and forensic science, were convinced he'd been murdered. If it had not been for her, some innocent person would now be languishing in a prison cell courtesy of forensic sciences like fingerprinting, so terribly discredited in recent years. Perhaps she communicates, not with a dead person, but with some form of energy that is left behind. A soul, perhaps? Think about that. You have heard evidence from some of the most eminent theologians and philosophers in the world. Buddhists, Christians, Sikhs, Muslims, Hindus and many more. Many of them are at odds with each other and disagree about many things but all of them – all of them! – believe there is some form of life after death. Every major religion in the world believes there is an afterlife. They only disagree on what particular form it might take.'

I watched the jury closely as Paul strode around the court like some religious evangelist and was mesmerised by the sheer theatrical performance of it all.

'In most theological and philosophical traditions,' he was off again, 'the concept of life as a cycle of birth, death and

186

being born again is assumed or accepted as a fact of nature. No scientist of any note would fundamentally challenge the first two elements of the cyclical process, but for thousands of years the concept of being born again has fostered debate and disagreement among scientists, theologians and philosophers. To some thinkers, the idea of being born again means that following death, there is an afterlife where a person or part of a person, sometimes referred to as a soul or a spirit, ascends or descends into Heaven or Hell for eternity, never to return to this earth. Others postulate that dead people, or their spirits, will at some point return to earth for some form of final judgement or apocalyptic battle, following which some will ascend to a paradise, be thrown into hell or be reborn and live again to re-populate the earth. Other religious, philosophical or mystical beliefs propose that the dead return to some higher or lower form of existence largely determined by the moral quality of their previous earth life. This is often referred to as transmigration, where a dead person may return as another human being or an animal. A fourth option in the debate about what happens after death, proposes that there is a rebirth or reincarnation and the dead person will return to earth as a new human being.

Of course, there are many variations on these beliefs, but a common theme is that death by itself is never final. Belief in reincarnation or some other form of rebirth has existed ever since the days of the ancient Egyptians and perhaps before that. The personal possessions buried with the dead in the ancient tombs evidence that there was a belief that there would be a need for them in some other life. As we move through the ages, to the modern day, we learn that reincarnation in some form or another has been a core part of many religious and philosophical beliefs. This belief stems from the concept that in simple terms, man has a soul or spirit that can be transferred to another new life. Ancient Greek philosophers such as Pythagoras, Socrates and Plato, proposed the idea of reincarnation. The ancient Orphic religion taught that the soul is immortal, divine and aspires to freedom, but is enchained by the body until death, when it is released only to be re-imprisoned in another body in order to maintain the birth, death, rebirth cycle. Other ancient religions and philosophies describe similar beliefs including Jewish mystics, Gnostics and the early American and Inuit Indians. In the modern world, the concept of reincarnation is found in many Indian philosophies and religions, Hindu, Sikhism, Buddhism, and others. It is also found in some African religions, among modern pagans, in Norse mythology and in the New Age movement. In some form or another, almost all ancient and modern philosophies and religions tend towards an acceptance of birth, death and some form of rebirth or reincarnation.'

Stopping briefly for a moment to sip from a glass of water, Paul eyed the jury over the top of the glass and after he placed it deliberately on the table, he continued in the manner reminiscent of an old university professor passing on his understanding and perceptions of life to his beloved students. Speaking in plain, simple English he began to outline case after case where children had told researchers of their life in another time and place. A life before their present existence. A young boy who described life with a family on a remote Scottish island that neither he nor any of his present family had ever visited. The boy gave the names of his former parents and his brothers and sisters as well as describing the house he lived in down to the type of flowers in the garden and what life was like living in the small island community. Facts that were later verified by independent research and which the boy could never have learned from other members of his family, friends, books or a television programme. Another young lad related his former life as an American airplane pilot shot down by the Japanese in 1945. He described many attributes of different types of aircraft and explained step by step the pre-flight checks carried out by pilots when he was only four years old. Another boy told of his former life as his own grandfather, showing researchers birthmarks consistent in size, shape and colour with the scars his grandfather had been left with from childhood injuries and a war wound.

'None of these cases,' he told the jury, 'have any scientific explanation; none were proven to be fake, fantasy or mental aberrations. Science could offer no answer!'

He did not confine himself to cases involving children but also spoke at length about adults who claimed to have gone through what he called a 'near-death experience'. Mostly these were people who had technically died when they were being medically operated on, or as a result of some sort of accident. They claimed they floated above their own bodies and were able to witness the events below. In many examples, according to witnesses, the person could not have physically seen what they claimed to have seen, simply because of where their physical bodies were situated at the time. In other cases the person relating the experience was blind and could see nothing prior to their 'death'. When you weeded out the fakers, fantasists and phonies no explanation could be offered for the others. Quoting the great detective Sherlock Holmes, Thornton told the jury,

'When you eliminate the impossible, whatever remains – however improbable – must be the truth.'

After relating many sworn examples of reincarnation and near-death experience without the aid of notes, Paul continued,

'Science cannot explain these, so it simply says reincarnation does not exist. We are born, we procreate our own species, and

189

we die. That is their materialist view. Matter is all that matters. Matter is the only thing that exists. Everything that exists is composed of physical material and if it is not, then it does not exist. Even our dreams are composed of a substance: energy. When the brain dies, there is no energy and thus according to science, nothing can exist beyond death. To them, the brain and the mind are one entity, so when the brain dies, the mind dies also. Apart from their position being wholly beyond proof, they adhere to it like it was a sacred cow. Despite the vastness of our universe, most of them believe we are the only thinking life form that exists. A position of the highest form of arrogance; a godlike, "holier than thou" view. This, from the people who exploded the first atomic bomb without ever understanding how it truly worked. They could have blown the whole world apart for all they knew, but their egotistical nature drove them on towards destroying the earth and everything in it. They develop materials for use as biological and chemical weapons, to satisfy their own curiosities and like spoiled little children, cannot leave things alone.'

It was clear that he was coming near the end of his speech, during which the prosecuting counsel had sat silently, but demonstratively shaking his head or pretending to sigh deeply in an attempt to ridicule or show his disdain for some of the points raised by the defence. Frankly, I felt his actions were to an extent alienating the jury, some of whom I detected were in fact enjoying Thornton's gentle diatribe against the scientific profession. But even although most of us like to see supercilious types brought down a peg or two, I mused that that wouldn't necessarily be enough to convince this or any other panel of judges to set me free. I shrugged off my negative thoughts and returned my attention to Thornton, who was still on his feet.

'You have heard a great deal of evidence from various

witnesses,' he was saying, 'all of it points only in one direction. George Giles died in Italy, on the morning of the 17th July 1945 at 09:50 hours. He was killed by a stray landmine on the side of a road near the Italian town of Orsogna.'

Suddenly he stopped speaking and began to sing softly:

'They were singing Tipperary as they marched on down the road,

They were singing of the joys of going home

They were singing Tipperary then I heard the bomb explode

Then the silence and I knew that they were gone.'

He stopped and for a moment eyed each of the jury in turn. Then in a quiet voice he began:

'That song was written by a soldier who witnessed George Giles and his colleagues die. It was found in the records of the enquiry into the explosion. At precisely the same moment, according to his certificate of birth, Pietro Hunter was born in a village a few miles away. His father was a British soldier serving in Italy. After the war, he returned to Britain with his newborn son. His Italian wife would not leave her home in Italy and the young child was never to see his mother again. On that fateful day in 1945, the spirit of George Giles resided in the body of that young child who later became Peter Hunter, a psychotic killer. As Hunter grew up, he adopted the characteristics of evil that each of us have within us, but that which we rarely acknowledge. The Mr Hyde, if I can use my learned friend's earlier analogy. Fifty-five years later, when Hunter fell from the wall trying to escape from Broadmoor, he was rushed to hospital. The medical records show that he died in the back of the ambulance taking him there. Although the documents confirm he was technically dead, the skills of the medical team, using modern drugs and equipment, enabled him to be brought back to life. At some point in this birth-death-rebirth process, Mr Hyde was ousted by Dr Jekyll and when George Giles became conscious in hospital, he had been transported fifty-five years into the future. The mind, soul, spirit and consciousness of George Giles in 1945 had returned to occupy the body of Peter Hunter in the year 2000. Peter Hunter, ladies and gentlemen, now roams the universe seeking a host. Let us hope he never finds one. The man you see before you is George Giles. Psychiatry and psychology are relatively new branches of science. Faith, the belief that good should always triumph over evil and the conviction of life after death – these are the foundation stones of every major religion in the world and have been with us for thousands of years. Science has never proven that death is a final end. In this case, good has triumphed over evil, but if you send my client back to Broadmoor, you do the Devil's work. He has committed no crime before man or God, and it is your duty to say that to be so. I am sure you will not shrink from that duty for fear of ridicule, scorn or derision. Death does not bring an end to a person's life; it is a gate through which the consciousness departs from one life and begins the journey to another. Thank you.'

He walked slowly back to our table, sat down and sipped the water from his glass. I knew it was almost over. Only the judge's summing up was to come and then the long wait for the verdict after the jury retired to their deliberations. After Thornton sat down, the judge ordered a short adjournment and for about fifteen minutes I sat alone with my thoughts, save for the guards at my back. When the proceedings resumed the judge summed up the evidence in as fair and impartial way as anyone could have done under the circumstances. He made it clear that whether I was Peter Hunter or George Giles was a matter for the jury. Where he felt the evidence of either side could not be supported by known facts, he was not afraid to say so and in the end I felt he presented a very balanced address to the jury and I found it impossible to assess his personal opinion. When he had finished speaking, I watched as one by one the men and women left the jury box and made their way to the jury room to decide my future. I turned to Paul and told him I didn't feel that I wanted to be in court when they came back with their verdict and asked if I could be taken to the cell below and hear the news from him later.

'I really can't bear to look at their faces as they come back,' I said. 'I'll try to read their thoughts and work out how they voted before the verdict is given. I really can't face it.'

He nodded his understanding and it was arranged for me to return to my cell downstairs.

CHAPTER TWENTY-THREE

A week after the case ended, I was being driven north to David's flat in Glasgow. Paul Thornton, the man who only liked hard cases, the man who believed a lawyer was either a social engineer or a parasite on society, had pulled it off. Despite the odds, he'd convinced the jury that on the balance of probabilities I was George Giles, a man who had come back from the dead to find rebirth in the body of another. David was driving and seated next to him was Father Flaherty who was going to Scotland to take in some fishing. Alongside me in the back of the car sat Reverend Jean Robinson, making her way back to Glasgow and her flock.

After the jury had returned their verdict, David had come into the cell with as broad a smile as I'd ever seen on a human being's face. He looked up at the little window before he spoke:

'For he who lives more lives than one – more deaths than one must die.'

He smiled at me before saying, 'Oscar Wilde. Wonderful stuff! Congratulations, George. You are a free man! Well, almost free. We have to find a way to get you out of here. There's an army of reporters outside, desperate for your statement, but all in good time.'

What happened next, I can barely remember. Everything went so quickly. The small cell filled up with official-looking people with documents for me to sign, after which I was bundled through a crowd of people into the back of a police van which drove away at high speed. We were escorted by police motorcycles and two other cars pursued by a fleet of vehicles carrying journalists and television crews. In the back of the van I was given a policeman's uniform to change into and when we arrived at a police station in North London, one of the police officers wearing my clothes was bundled into the office with a blanket over his head. An hour or so later I walked calmly past the crowd of waiting reporters, stepped into a police car along with another officer and we drove off without any of them batting an eyelid.

In the days that followed the trial, offers had poured in for me to appear on radio and television; there was talk of a film and David had already started work on his book. I was invited to do lecture tours around the world, submit articles, open buildings, judge competitions and take part in all sorts of events: the list was not exhaustive. In fact, it was all too much to deal with and David and I agreed to sneak off to Scotland to take some time to think things over and work on David's book.

It was early on Saturday morning when we left London in our small hire car and set off up the M1 just after five o'clock. We were joined by Jean, who had remained in London promoting her work in a series of interviews on radio and television. We made good time on the motorway and stopped for some refreshments near Preston. After an enjoyable lunch and a good old gossip about this and that we left the motorway service station just as it began to rain heavily. A few miles north parts of the motorway had begun to flood when we reached the border. Just after Gretna Green, we were overtaken by a large truck that sent a mucky spray across the windscreen and windows. David was blinded for a few seconds and when he tried to roll down his window he lost control, and the car aquaplaned into the central barrier on the carriageway. It bounced off the barrier like a snooker ball off a cushion and back across the road into the oncoming traffic. I remember it rolled from side to side when it was hit from behind by another truck, causing it to overturn and skid along the road on its roof.

The last view I had before I passed out was of the world upside down.

***

I awoke in a hospital ward but I instantly recognised it wasn't Broadmoor. I had a blinding headache, but everything else seemed to be okay. As I felt around, my arms and legs seemed fine and I could move them without difficulty. I pushed myself upright and had a look around the room but there was nothing unusual: it was a normal hospital ward. A nurse entered the room and she was slightly startled when she saw I was awake.

'Ah, you've come back to us. How do you feel?'

'I feel fine,' I said. 'Just a bit of a headache, that's all. Where am I?'

'You're in hospital,' she said, stating the obvious.

'I realise that,' I replied heatedly, 'but where?'

'Dumfries General Infirmary, in Scotland. You were brought here after the accident.'

'Scotland! Accident!' I thought. None of this made sense. I had no recollection of why I was in Scotland or of being involved in an accident, but I decided against saying anything and allowed her to continue without interruption.

'You were in a car accident. You and your colleagues were on your way to Scotland when your car overturned. You were all very lucky to get away with concussion and some minor injuries.'

'Colleagues? What colleagues?'

'Perhaps you're suffering from a bit of amnesia. It'll come

back to you. Now, you have a rest and I'll fetch you a cup of tea. The doctor will be round soon.'

I watched her leave and was surprised to notice that she didn't lock the room door after her. I swung my legs over the bed and sat upright. I was steady enough on my feet and walked over to the door.

I put my ear to the door and listened, but everything was quiet, save the low hum of the air conditioning. I turned the handle and gently pulled the door open. I looked right and left along the corridor but there was no activity. At the far end to my left, I could see a large glass double door with a sign above it reading 'Accident and Emergency'. The rear of an ambulance came into view and two people opened the ambulance doors and a third helped a man down the steps into the arms of the waiting nurses. This was the main door in and out of the emergency department. I was on the ground floor and less than a hundred feet from freedom. Just as I was considering my next move, a door in the corridor opened and the nurse I'd spoken with earlier appeared and walked hurriedly in my direction.

'Were you looking for something?' she asked.

'Nothing in particular.' I said. 'Just making myself familiar with the surroundings.'

'That door,' she said, pointing to where the ambulance was parked, 'leads to the outside. The door at the other end takes you to the canteen. There's a smoke room inside the canteen.'

'I don't smoke.'

'Very wise,' she responded, in a patronising tone.

She guided me back into my room, speaking as we moved. 'Dr Campbell is arranging another brain scan for this afternoon. Provided everything is clear and there are no complications, you could be discharged in the morning.'

'Discharged? You mean I'll be free to leave?'

'Of course! Why ever would we want to keep you here?

Over the course of the next hour, I had a rather bland lunch in the canteen before returning to my room. I was seated at the window when I heard a knock at the door. 'Trolley! Trolley!' a voice called out.

'Come in!' I replied and the door opened, revealing a woman standing in the corridor with a trolley that held sweets, juice, crisps and newspapers. 'Do you want anything?' she asked.

'Can I have a newspaper? Any one will do.'

She handed me a folded paper and I paid for it with some coins lying on a cabinet at the side of the bed. I settled back in the chair and thumbed through the paper, but found its contents decidedly dull and threw it onto the bed. On the top of the small bedside cabinet, I noticed a brown suede wallet. Inside there were some plastic cards and other bits and pieces. It appeared to belong to George Giles. I opened the drawer at the top of the cabinet and removed some letters, cards and a couple of official-looking documents and lay back on the bed to read them. They also belonged to George Giles and I struggled to try and remember if I knew someone by that name. Nothing I recalled from the past was of any help and my memory of recent events wasn't too clear. A sudden tiredness engulfed me and I lay down on the bed and fell asleep.

I awoke with a start at the sound of the nurse entering the room. She fussed around with some of the equipment, changed the water in the jug by my bedside, poured some into a glass and handed it to me with a couple of pills. She worked in silence and as I watched her I was reminded of some other young women. The memories were vague but I recalled a nurse, a trainee accountant, shop assistant, a flower seller, a hairdresser, a prostitute and a young girl who worked with computers.

'The radiator doesn't work properly,' the nurse said. 'The maintenance man says there's something wrong with the thermostat. If you hit it a couple of times, it switches itself on. He's coming back to look at it tomorrow.'

I saw under the radiator there were a couple of tools left lying. Among them a familiar hard-faced, ball-peen hammer. The nurse had her back to me and was smoothing the bed sheets when I turned round with the hammer in my hand.

Some other books from Ringwood Publishing

All titles are available from the Ringwood website (including first edition signed copies) and from usual outlets.
Also available in Kindle, Kobo and Nook.
www.ringwoodpublishing.com

Ringwood Publishing, 7 Kirklee Quadrant, Glasgow, G12 0TS

mail@ringwoodpublishing.com
0141 357-6872

Morbid Relations
Jonathan Whitelaw

Morbid Relations is the story of Rob Argyll, an unsuccessful stand-up comedian. Following his mother's death, he returns for the first time in years to his family in their Glasgow home. Rob struggles to relate to his somewhat dysfunctional family, seeming to bounce from one mistake to another while simultaneously trying to make amends for his long absence. The narrative is a darkly comic take on modern Scottish life, family relationships, and finally trying to grow up.

ISBN: 978-1-901514-19-3   £9.99

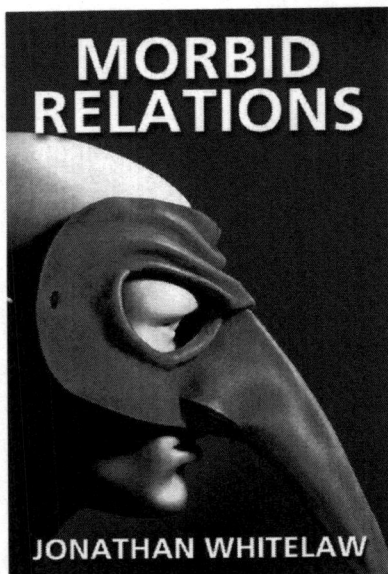

Memoirs of a Feminist Mother

Carol Fox

As a committed feminist, Carol Fox has achieved success for very many women, but her greatest battle described in this book was very personal. Following serious fertility problems, Carol made the positive decision to become a single parent by choice, to have a child while she still could. Refused access to fertility treatment in Scotland she had no choice but to move to London. Through sheer determination and tenacity, Carol obtained treatment in England in the early 1990s and her daughter was born in 1992, following extensive fertility treatment and battles against judgemental attitudes which appear almost vindictive to us 25 years later. Her story has attracted media coverage, sparking debates on motherhood and the right to be a single parent in the UK.

ISBN: 978-1-901514-21-6   £9.99

The Malta Job

Alywn James

The Malta Job follows the story of John Smith, a young Scottish journalist with literary aspirations, who is sent to Malta to complete a sequel to the very successful MacMurder, a round-up of Scotland's more infamous homicides. Once on Malta, with the dead author's notes, he gets involved in a gripping set of circumstances involving high romance, exciting adventure and a bank heist crime.

ISBN: 978-1-901514-17-9   £9.99

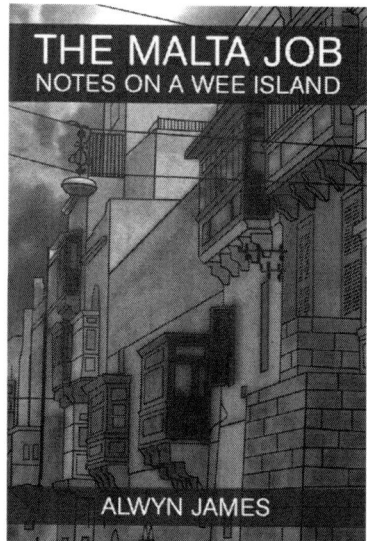

Calling Cards

Gordon Johnston

Calling Cards is a psychological crime thriller set in Glasgow about stress, trauma, addiction, recovery, denial and corruption.

Following an anonymous email Journalist Frank Gallen and DI Adam Ralston unravel a web of corruption within the City Council with links to campaign against a new housing development in Kelvingrove Park and the frenzied attacks of a serial killer. They then engage in a desperate chase to identify a serial killer from the clues he is sending them.

ISBN: 978-1-901514-09-4   £9.99

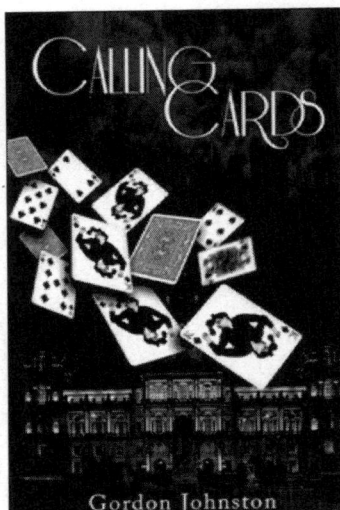

A Subtle Sadness

Sandy Jamieson

A Subtle Sadness follows the life of Frank Hunter and is an exploration of Scottish Identity and the impact on it of politics, football, religion, sex and alcohol.

It covers a century of Scottish social, cultural and political highlights culminating in Glasgow's emergence in 1990 as European City of Culture.

It is not a political polemic but it puts the current social, cultural and political debates in a recent historical context.

ISBN: 978-1-901514-04-9   £9.99

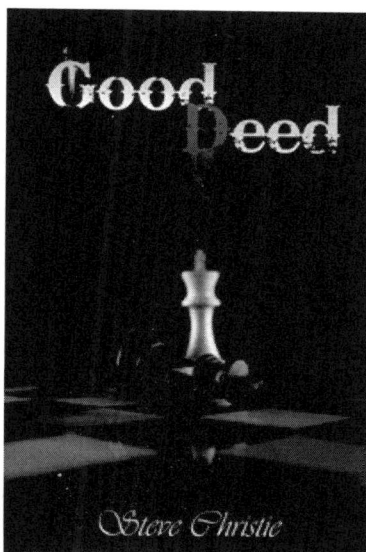

Good Deed

Steve Christie

Good Deed introduces a new Scottish detective hero, DI Ronnie Buchanan.

It was described by one reviewer as *"Christopher Brookmyre on speed, with more thrills and less farce"*.

The events take Buchanan on a frantic journey around Scotland as his increasingly deadly pursuit of a mysterious criminal master mind known only as Vince comes to a climax back in Aberdeen.

ISBN: 978-1-901514-06-3   £9.99

Dark Loch

Charles P. Sharkey

Dark Loch is an epic tale of the effects of the First World War on the lives of the residents of a small Scottish rural community. The main characters are the tenant crofters who work the land leased to them by the Laird. The crofters live a harsh existence in harmony with the land and the changing seasons, unaware of the devastating war that is soon to engulf the continent of Europe.

The book vividly and dramatically explores the impact of that war on all the main characters and how their lives are drastically altered forever.

ISBN: 978-1-901514-14-8   £9.99

Black Rigg

Mary Easson

Black Rigg is set in a Scottish mining village in the year 1910 in a period of social and economic change. Working men and women began to challenge the status quo but landowners, the church and the justice system resisted. Issues such as class, power, injustice, poverty and community are raised by the narrative in powerful and dramatic style.

ISBN: 978-1-901514-15-5   £9.99

Torn Edges

Brian McHugh

Torn Edges is a mystery story linking modern day Glasgow with 1920's Ireland and takes a family back to the tumultuous days of the Irish Civil War.

They soon learn that many more Irishman were killed, murdered or assassinated during the very short Civil War than in the War of Independence and that gruesome atrocities were committed by both sides.

The evidence begins to suggest that their own relatives might have been involved.

ISBN: 978-1-901514-05-6   £9.99

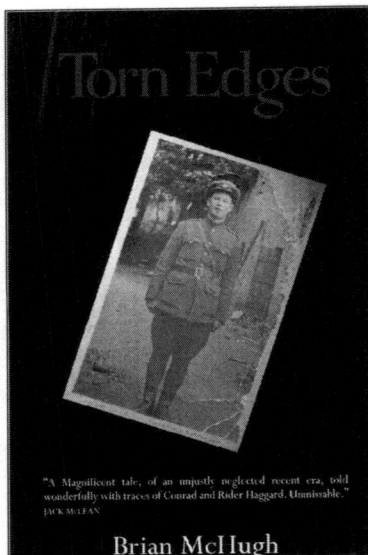

"A Magnificent tale, of an unjustly neglected recent era, told wonderfully with traces of Conrad and Rider Haggard. Unmissable."
JACK McLEAN

Brian McHugh

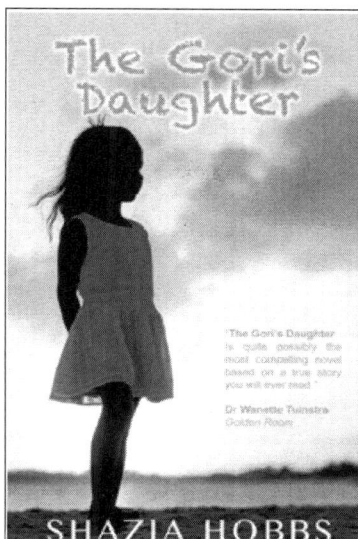

The Gori's Daughter
Shazia Hobbs

The Gori's Daughter is the story of Aisha, a young mixed race woman, daughter of a Kashmiri father and a Glasgow mother. Her life is a struggle against rejection and hostility in Glasgow's white and Asian communities.

The book documents her fight to give her own daughter a culture and tradition that she can accept with pride. The tale is often harrowing but is ultimately a victory for decency over bigotry and discrimination.

ISBN: 978-1-901514-12-4   £9.99

Scotball
Stephen O'Donnell

Scotball is a searing examination of the current state of Scottish football and the various social, political and economic forces that combine to strangle its integrity and potential.

ISBN: 978-1-901514-13-1   £9.99

Paradise Road
Stephen O'Donnell

Paradise Road is the story of Kevin McGarry, who through a combination of injury and disillusionment is forced to abandon any thoughts of playing football professionally. Instead he settles for following his favourite team, Glasgow Celtic, whilst trying to eke out a living as a joiner. It considers the role of young working-class men in our post-industrial society.

ISBN: 978-1-901514-07-0   £9.99